SALTWATER COWBOY

SALTWATER COWBOYS, BOOK 1

CHRISTY BARRITT

Copyright © 2020 by Christy Barritt

All rights reserved.

No part of this book may be reproduced in any form or by any electronic or mechanical means, including information storage and retrieval systems, without written permission from the author, except for the use of brief quotations in a book review.

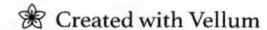

❦ Created with Vellum

CHAPTER ONE

"BOBBY, DON'T DO IT." As Dani Dodson stared at the gun pointed at her, a tremble raked through her.

The wind swept across their boat, and the waves violently rocked the vessel. In the distance, lightning cracked the inky black sky, reminding her she was in the middle of nowhere.

They should have never come out on the water this evening.

Then again, if Dani had a choice, she wouldn't be in this situation at all. Bobby had forced her to get onboard this boat. The bruise on her cheek was a grim reminder of what would happen if she didn't comply.

"Look, Dani. I'm sorry." Bobby raked a hand through his hair as his tortured eyes begged for her forgiveness.

She gripped the side of the boat, her broken nails digging into the wet metal. As the vessel jostled again, she lurched backward.

The air left her lungs as she felt herself start to fall backward.

Before she tumbled overboard, the boat rocked and her feet sank back onto the deck.

She didn't have time to feel relieved. Instead, her gaze snapped back to the gun in Bobby's hand.

The one aimed right at her chest. Coupled with the tortured look in the man's eyes, Dani knew she was in deep trouble. This wasn't going to end well.

"There's got to be another way." Her voice quivered as the words flew from her lips. "I won't tell anyone your secret. I promise."

Rain saturated their faces. Any area of skin left dry by the rain was claimed by the spray of the waves or the sheen of adrenaline-fueled sweat.

"Bobby!" one of his friends called from the boat's cabin. "We gotta get out of here. The storm is getting worse, and we're not going to make it much longer."

Bobby turned back to her, and Dani saw his gaze harden with decision. "I'm sorry, Dani. You left me with no choice."

"Wait—"

But before she could say anything else, a bang exploded in the air.

Pain pierced her skin. Her muscles. Maybe even her bones.

The momentum of the blast knocked her off her feet, and Dani flailed through the air.

The twenty-seven previous years of her life bombarded her thoughts. Mostly her mistakes. If only she had a chance to go back to make things right, to make better choices, to use more wisdom.

Dani knew that wouldn't be the case.

As her body collided with the angry ocean, waves consumed her, and everything went black.

CHAPTER TWO

LEVI SUTHERLAND RODE his mare to the top of the sand dune and paused. "Whoa, Nelly."

He smiled as he said the words. They never got old. He hadn't given the horse that name—his father had. But the moniker had stuck and become somewhat of a running joke in his family.

Levi glanced over the stretch of sand that led to the mighty Atlantic Ocean.

Evidence of last night's storm was visible in the weathered landscape. What a storm it had been. Thunder had rattled walls. Lightning had flickered like silent threats from all directions. Still today, puddles marred the sandy roads of Cape Corral.

The eight thousand acre barrier island stretched off the coast of North Carolina, near the state line bordering Virginia. A two-lane bridge led to the secluded isle, which was also a horse sanctuary. However, that bridge had been washed out three weeks ago when a nor'easter came through. Crews were working hard to make it functional again. In the meantime, people had to travel to the island either by boat or, for a lucky few, helicopter.

As Levi waited, his phone rang. He pulled the device from his pocket and saw the familiar name. Frowning, he put the cell to his ear. "Hey, Langston. Or should I say Mayor Hughes?"

"Whichever one makes you more inclined to accept my offer. You thought any more about what you want to do?"

Levi's frown deepened. "I have been thinking about it, but I haven't made a decision."

"I can wait a week. But, if you say no, I need to look elsewhere. We'd love to have you as the new police chief here in Kernersville. You'd have eighty people under you, and it would definitely be a step up from your little island."

Levi couldn't deny the truth in Langston's words. But he wasn't sure he wanted to leave this place either. "I'll have an answer for you by the end of the week. You have my word."

"I know a Sutherland promise is as good as gold."

"That's how my parents raised me."

"And one more reason why I want you here in my town. You were meant to do more than act as a saltwater cowboy. You're wasting your talent on that small island. I do hope you'll make the right choice."

As Levi put his phone away, he hoped the same thing. Though he loved Cape Corral, he couldn't deny how nice it would be sometimes to get away from all the bad memories.

He had a lot of thinking to do.

With a sigh, Levi continued to scan the shoreline. To his left, three SUVs were parked near the water, and their passengers had already pulled out their fishing poles. People often came here to vacation and enjoy some of the serenity the island offered.

His gaze traveled to the right as he searched for the island's wild horses.

There were at least four hundred of them on this sandy stretch of land. Tradition said a group of Spaniards was traveling across the ocean nearly five hundred years ago when their ship capsized nearby. The horses managed to escape to what was now known as Cape Corral and had been here wandering the shores ever since.

By law, the animals were protected. But that didn't mean that people didn't do stupid things sometimes. That also didn't mean that these horses didn't, on occasion, need a hand with a disease or an injury. That was where Levi and his men came in.

Levi clucked his tongue and lightly nudged Nelly's side. "Come on, girl."

She started toward the beach. At any time, Levi expected to see the wild horses. Sometimes, they liked to roll in the water to begin the day, especially if it was hot outside. Other times, a whole herd would stampede down the shoreline. The sight still took his breath away.

Nelly's hooves hit the soft sand as they patrolled the beach. Several pieces of driftwood had washed ashore last night, along with a greater than usual amount of seaweed. Unbroken whelk shells tumbled in the waves, as well as some Scotch bonnets and a few mermaid's purses, as tourists like to call them.

The scent of the sea rose up around him—briny, fishy, salty. Mixed with the smell of his horse, the aromas signified home.

Just ahead, Levi spotted the harem of horses he'd been looking for.

"The divas have arrived," he murmured to Nelly.

He liked to call the three mares the Mean Girls. Not that the horses themselves were mean—though they could be. But these three mares liked to stay to themselves. They rarely accepted any other horses into their clique, and the way they raised their heads sometimes made it appear they thought they were better than the rest.

They were out for their morning stroll today, their stallion, Scar, walking behind them.

Levi and Nelly trotted toward them. His job was to monitor the animals and make sure they remained healthy and safe.

Something up ahead caught his eye, something that had washed up in the storm last night.

Levi clucked his tongue again. "Let's get a little closer, Nelly."

The debris almost looked like a blanket being tossed in the shore break.

But Levi didn't think that's what it was.

As he got closer, a mass of dark hair came into focus.

His heart pounded harder. "Oh, no . . ."

Was that a . . . woman?

His breath caught as the truth washed over him.

It was.

His gaze jerked toward the Mean Girls again.

Though Scar ran along the shore, the mares were stampeding right toward this woman.

In less than thirty seconds, the horses would trample her.

Levi had to think of a way to stop them, and he had no time to waste.

"Let's go, Nelly. Now!"

CHAPTER THREE

LEVI NUDGED his foot into Nelly's side again. "Faster, girl. Faster."

Only a few more feet, and Levi would reach the woman.

His throat tightened as he realized this may not have a happy ending.

The Mean Girls were dangerously close.

Dear Lord ... help us now. Please.

Making a split-second decision, Levi pulled the reins. Nelly stopped beside the woman.

They formed a barrier between the horses and this woman.

Levi braced himself.

The Mean Girls *should* go around him.

He hoped.

Dear Lord, Your assistance would be great any time now.

The approaching horses sounded like thunder as their hooves pounded across the shore.

The Mean Girls still charged toward them, undeterred by Levi.

Nelly whined and pranced in place.

"It's okay, girl," Levi murmured before waving his hands in the air, trying to scare the harem out of the way.

Only three feet stretched between him and a possible collision.

He held his breath.

Finally, the mares split and crossed on either side of him.

As they continued to thunder down the shore, Levi released his breath and wiped a hand across his brow.

That had been too close.

Wasting no time, Levi climbed off Nelly and knelt beside the woman.

Blood soaked her chest, and her figure appeared lifeless, limp as the waves that lapped over her jean-clad legs.

Levi pressed his finger into the side of the woman's neck.

A faint heartbeat pounded there.

She was still alive!

But barely. That blood around her left shoulder ... it appeared to be from a gunshot wound.

He grabbed his radio. This woman needed medical help ASAP. Levi quickly called the situation in, and dispatch promised to send assistance.

Putting his radio away, he leaned closer to the woman. Levi gently turned her on her right side. As he did, the woman coughed. Water gushed from her mouth.

A few coughs later, she groaned. "Please . . . help me."

"It's going to be okay." Levi leaned closer to her.

Her eyes popped open. Fear slashed their depths, like someone awaking from a nightmare.

As her gaze fell on Levi, the fear seemed to dissipate.

For a moment.

The next instant, her face squeezed with pain. She reached for Levi, desperation in her gaze.

"Don't let them get me." She clutched his shirt with a surprising strength. "Please, don't let them find me."

With those last words, her eyes closed and she slipped into unconsciousness again.

What was she talking about?

Levi didn't know.

He just prayed that help got here in time.

"I HEARD YOU WERE HERE."

Levi looked over and saw Grant Matthews, one of his colleagues with Forestry Law Enforcement, standing in the doorway of the waiting room at the Cape Corral Medical Center.

"Hey, thanks for coming." Levi realized he was slouching in the uncomfortable plastic seat and sat up straighter.

"How'd you even get here? I didn't see your truck outside—or Nelly."

"My truck is in the shop, so my sister brought me by. Emmy needed to stop by the post office anyway."

Levi stretched out his legs and tried to push away the bad memories that came with the sterile scent of these sanitized walls. With the familiar sounds of padded footsteps and murmured voices whispering about life and death. With the bone-crushing uncertainty that pressed the air.

This wasn't the time to mourn Adrienne. The best thing he could do was to focus on the present —on the woman who'd washed ashore.

Normally, someone like the person Levi found today would be taken to a bigger medical facility in a nearby metropolitan area. But with the bridge leading to the island washed out, the island doctor had agreed to look at their Jane Doe.

Grant stepped farther into the small waiting

room, which was empty other than the two of them. "What's all the hullabaloo about?"

Details from this morning rushed back to Levi. "An unidentified female washed up on shore. No ID. There haven't been any missing person reports or any indications of an incident out at sea during last night's storm."

Grant crossed his arms and leaned against the mauve-colored wall, a thoughtful expression on his face. "So where did she come from?"

"That's what I'm wondering as well."

"It's amazing she survived in those conditions. That storm last night was bad."

"And with a gunshot wound at that."

Grant's eyes widened. "A gunshot wound? This is growing more and more intriguing by the moment."

Levi nodded, unable to deny the truth in his words. "Isn't it? Maybe once she's awake, she'll be able to fill in some blanks. Lots of blanks."

Grant readjusted his cowboy hat. "What's the latest update on her?"

"Dr. Knightly is doing surgery to extract the bullet, but he should be done any time now."

Levi was thankful Dr. Knightly was here today. He only came to the island three days a week. Otherwise, the clinic was staffed with a nurse practitioner, two RNs, and three assistants.

Levi was anxious to hear if the woman was

okay. Something about her had just seemed so vulnerable, so lost. Levi hadn't been able to get her out of his mind.

"What happens after her surgery?" Grant asked. "We can't send her out all willy-nilly, right?"

Levi shifted in his seat. "We get her statement and call her next of kin."

Plus, the woman's words continued to haunt him.

Don't let them get me. Please, don't let them find me.

He rubbed his jaw at the memory.

What happened to the woman? She had to be around Levi's age. Her long dark hair flowed with saltwater-sprayed curls. Based on her designer jeans and fancy white blouse, she had money. Most people didn't wear jeans on boats, though. It was September, but the air was still warm on most days.

Yet she'd washed up from the ocean.

Levi had checked. There were no reports of any fishing vessels that had taken on water or called in an SOS.

So where had she come from?

"It's not every day something like this happens on Cape Corral," Grant muttered.

"No. I must say it's been pretty peaceful lately."

Grant lowered himself into the chair next to Levi. He wore a black T-shirt and his customary cowboy hat—similar to Levi's own outfit. Some people might think cowboy hats were just for show, but there was nothing better to keep the sun out of your eyes while monitoring the island.

"The calm before the storm?" Grant asked.

"Let's hope not."

Just then, the doctor stepped into the room. Levi stood, anxious to hear what he had to say.

CHAPTER FOUR

DR. KNIGHTLY TUCKED a clipboard beneath his arm as he paused in front of Levi and Grant. "This woman is a living, breathing miracle."

"So she's doing okay?" Levi wasn't sure why he felt unexplainably relieved. He'd worked with plenty of people who needed his help. Why did this woman feel different?

"I'd say she's doing more than okay. Somehow that bullet managed to miss any major arteries, organs, and bones. We essentially just had to remove the bullet, clean the wound, and stitch her up. Time will do the rest of the healing."

"That's great." Levi had expected far worse.

"But there's bad news also." The doctor paused and glanced at Levi then Grant, premature lines stretching across his tanned forehead. When the man wasn't working, he was an avid surfer. That made this job perfect for him. The island had plenty of opportunity to enjoy the ocean in between working.

Levi shifted, wondering exactly how bad this could get. "What's going on?"

Dr. Knightly rolled his shoulders back. "I'm probably saying too much, but the woman doesn't remember who she is."

"You mean she has amnesia?" Levi clarified, uncertain if he'd heard correctly. He'd never actually worked with someone who had lost their memory. He'd only heard about it, mostly on TV and in movies.

"That's correct. She can't recall the events leading up to her being here. She was wearing a necklace with 'Dani' in ornate letters across the front. We can only assume that's her first name."

"Is this normal?" Levi narrowed his eyes, feeling the knot that formed on his brow. "I don't know much about amnesia..."

"It's called dissociative amnesia, and it's usually brought on by trauma. Unfortunately, this disorder doesn't always fit into a box. It can have various degrees of severity that differ from victim to victim."

"Will she get her memory back?" Grant leaned forward, his brow also furrowed with thought.

Dr. Knightly shook his head, though the action seemed hesitant. "That's also iffy. I've read about cases where people do, and I've heard of cases where people don't. Not very hopeful, but it's the truth."

Levi let those facts sink in until another question rose to the surface. "What does this mean for her future? Without next of kin to call, what's the protocol here at the medical center?"

"Technically, we should be able to release her by this evening. There's nothing as far as her physical injuries to keep her here. But . . . I can't release someone who's not competent to take care of herself. It would be unethical."

Levi shifted. "So what are you going to do?"

"That's what I need to figure out," Dr. Knightly said. "Normally, it wouldn't be a problem. But I've got four people headed to the clinic right now."

"What happened?" Levi asked.

"They ate some bad shellfish—they cooked the dish themselves and apparently left their clams out in the sun for too long."

"That's unfortunate."

Dr. Knightly raised his eyebrows. "Especially since we have only four beds."

Levi's jaw tightened. "We're Cape Corral. We're a refuge for those who need it—be horse or human. We'll figure out something. In the meantime, can I talk to Dani?"

"Of course." The doctor shifted his clipboard to his other arm. "I told her you'd want to. Just be gentle with her. She's been through a lot and to say she's fragile right now would be an understatement."

Levi couldn't argue with that. He just prayed he had the right words to bring resolution to this situation.

DANI SUCKED in a breath as the door to her room opened. She halfway expected it to be the doctor again, coming to tell her bad news.

Instead, a man wearing a plaid shirt, jeans, and a black cowboy hat stood there. A badge was clipped to his brown leather belt, and his hands went to his hips, almost as if he owned the place.

He definitely wasn't a doctor. But he most assuredly held some kind of jurisdiction.

She blinked as she stared at the man. He seemed vaguely familiar. Was this the person who'd rescued her?

That had to be it. It was the only thing that made sense. He would need to take a statement from her.

As the man stepped closer, Dani pulled the sheet up higher, suddenly too aware of how vulnerable she was. Whatever happened to bring her here left her feeling empty and off-balance.

"Hi there." The man paused, his voice low and rumbling. "I'm Officer Levi Sutherland."

She licked her parched lips, realizing with a sickening nausea that the only thing she remembered was the present—the time after she'd woken up from surgery. Anything before that was a blur.

At least she knew her name. "I'm Dani . . . I think."

"Do you remember your last name, Dani?" He sounded prodding and curious but not pushy.

She appreciated his bedside manner.

"I wish I did." As Dani said the words out loud, she felt her world rocking and everything blurred again.

How was it possible that she didn't remember her name? Nor could she remember how she'd ended up in this hospital or what had happened to put her here. All the doctor had said was that it had been something traumatic.

Nausea rose in her as panic pulsed in her veins. Part of her felt lost in a vast sea of darkness, a place with no paths to explore or escape plans or signals as to where to go.

Only nothingness.

Dani's stomach churned harder. She clutched it, praying she didn't spew in front of the officer. She had to hold it together if she was going to get through this.

"Dani." Officer Sutherland stepped closer,

standing near her feet. He said her name slowly, almost as if he wanted to catch her before she disappeared into the very nothingness trying to submerge her.

Instead of focusing on the unknown, she took a better look at the man. He was concrete and real—a new memory she could hold on to.

The officer was undoubtably handsome. Dani would guess him to be her age or maybe a little older. With his cowboy boots, he almost looked more suited for a Texas ranch than he did the coast.

That was right. She was on an island. The doctor had told her that much.

Dani prayed her memories would return and that everything would start making more sense soon.

"Do you have any idea how you ended up on the beach?" Officer Sutherland studied her face as he stood at the foot of the bed.

Dani shook her head and hugged the sheet in front of her with her agile arm. "No. I'm sorry. I wish I could tell you more. Not just for your sake, but for mine too."

A frown tugged at his lips. He was disappointed also, wasn't he? It would be hard to figure out what happened to her if she couldn't recall anything.

"Has anyone shown up to . . . claim me? To help fill in the holes in my story?" Her throat burned as the words left her lips. Dani almost felt like a stray dog waiting for an owner or a friend to show up and make things better. The feeling made another round of acid rise in her.

"No, I'm sorry." Officer Sutherland's blue eyes seemed to glimmer with understanding and sympathy, almost as if he knew grief personally, as if he'd dived into it and nearly hadn't surfaced before. Dani had known that no would be the answer, but that didn't stop her heart from plunging. If nobody came for her, what would she do? Where would she go?

She had no ID, no money, no idea where she lived, and no car. The list could go on.

The whole situation made another round of hopelessness echo inside her. The feeling washed over her like a huge wave and threatened to pull her under. Only, this time, she might not wash to shore and be brought back to life.

Maybe she was okay with that.

Dani fisted her hands in front of her. She couldn't think like that. She had to be a fighter and push through this.

With time, things would get easier . . . she hoped.

"The doctor told me you suffered a gunshot wound." Officer Sutherland made the statement matter-of-factly, yet his voice remained soft and his gaze prodding.

Instinctively, Dani reached for her injured shoulder. It had been bandaged, and she had to wear a sling to keep the muscles in place. However, Dr. Knightly had reminded her, with a slight track up or down, that bullet could have hit a major artery or even her heart. Her current discomfort was actually a blessing in disguise.

"Why would someone shoot me?" she whispered. "And who?"

A dark blob remained at her periphery, and, no matter how hard she tried, she was unable to identify it.

"We're going to figure that out, ma'am," Officer Sutherland said.

She shook her head, wishing that the action would somehow snap her thoughts back in place. She knew it was never that easy, though.

Officer Sutherland stepped back. He almost appeared as if he wanted to say more. But what else was there to say when Dani couldn't remember anything?

Would she become the hospital's problem now? A ward of the town?

Another shiver raked through Dani, claiming all her muscles. Even her teeth chattered at the notion.

Before she could say anything, a loud bang sounded outside her door.

And suddenly, everything around her spun.

CHAPTER FIVE

LEVI SAW Dani's eyes glaze. Saw the tremble that began in her arms. Saw how her body tensed.

Someone had dropped a tray of food in the hallway. The loud clatter must have triggered something in Dani—some kind of subconscious memory.

Of gunfire maybe? It made sense.

Levi stepped closer and touched Dani's arm, trying to keep her grounded before a panic attack kicked in.

"Hey, it's okay," he murmured, careful to keep his voice gentle.

She continued to stoically stare straight ahead, almost as if frozen with fear. Her chest barely moved, as if she wasn't inhaling or exhaling. Her lips parted ever so slightly.

"Dani?" Levi leaned closer with concern.

Her eyes jerked from their stationary position. As she looked at him, tears trickled down her bruised cheek.

"Did you remember something?" he prodded.

She rubbed her throat, still looking jumpy and wired. "No . . . only fear. Pain. Desperation. But nothing concrete."

"Just give it some time." Levi realized his hand was still on her arm and he pulled it away, trying to remain professional.

The woman just looked so alone . . . and leaving her suffering in solitude seemed so heartless. But Levi had to remember his place. On this island, he was law enforcement.

Dani nodded, but her gaze still looked empty.

Levi stared at the woman and could tell by her expression that she was lost in a sea of nothingness.

He tried to put himself in her shoes. He couldn't imagine what it would be like to not even know where you lived or your last name—or who had almost killed you.

Compassion pounded inside him. He wished he could do something to help but . . . his options were limited.

Finally, Levi cleared his throat. "Look, maybe you should stay in Cape Corral for a while. Maybe something here on the island will trigger a memory."

Something lit in her gaze. It wasn't excitement, but maybe . . . hope? Levi couldn't be sure.

"Maybe . . . but where would I stay? I . . . I don't want to be an inconvenience." Her gaze fluttered with uncertainty.

Levi didn't have to think long about his answer. "My sister runs an inn. You can stay there for a few days until you get back on your feet."

Dani stared at him. "Are you sure?"

"I'm positive."

Finally, Dani nodded. "Okay. If you don't mind, I'll take you up on that offer—at least until my family or friends get here. Hopefully, that will be soon."

Levi offered another stiff nod before stepping back. "Since that's settled, I'm going to be in the waiting room until the doctor clears you to leave."

"I'll . . . I'll repay you for any expenses you incur. As soon as I remember who I am, of course."

"I'm not worried about that. You just focus on getting better. The rest of the details will fall into place."

"Thank you, Officer Sutherland."

"Just call me Levi."

A quick but grateful smile tugged at her lips. "Okay then. Levi. Thank you."

With a nod goodbye, he stepped out the door and found Grant in the waiting area. "I hope you don't mind sticking around for a little bit longer."

Grant stood, hanging his thumbs in his pockets. "What's going on?"

"Our victim is going to stay in Cape Corral for a few days."

"She remembered something?"

Levi shook his head, wishing that was the case. This whole investigation would be a lot easier if she did. "No, she didn't. I'm hoping if she sees the beach—the area where she was found—that maybe it will trigger something."

Grant studied him for a minute. "If that's the case, then she's going to need somewhere to stay. Have you thought about that?"

"I haven't really thought about any of this." Levi took his hat off and ran a hand through his hair. "But Emmy has a room open at the inn. I'm going to talk to her."

Grant's eyes narrowed with thought. "Seems like you're going above and beyond for this woman."

"If I was in her shoes, I'd want someone to do the same for me. Besides, it's just a place to sleep for a little while. In the grand scheme of things, it's not really a big deal."

Grant continued to study Levi's face. The two were practically brothers, and Grant had been there for Levi during some of the worst times of his life. His loyalty wasn't something a person easily forgot.

"Are you sure this doesn't have anything to do with Adrienne?" Grant asked quietly.

At the sound of his deceased wife's name, an ache returned to Levi's heart, almost like it had never left. Probably because it hadn't, even after three years.

"I'm not saying anything," Levi said. "All I want to do is help someone who needs a hand. I can't leave her to fend for herself. Don't get me wrong—I know our job means that we shouldn't get involved. We do our duties, and we move on. At least, that's what they tell us."

"Your dad is the one who used to always preach that."

Levi couldn't argue with that. His dad had been a Wildlife Law Enforcement Officer here for many years. But a heart attack had put him out of commission five years ago. Now the man was attempting to enjoy his retirement.

But anything that didn't require work didn't seem worth doing when it came to Levi's father. That was one of the reasons his dad had gone down to South Carolina two weeks ago. Levi's uncle had knee replacement surgery, and Levi's dad had insisted on helping him out with his moving business as he recovered.

Levi tried to put those thoughts out of his head. Especially thoughts of Adrienne.

But being in this clinic . . . it raised all kinds of memories. Memories he'd like to forget.

For now, Levi just needed to think about getting through this day. That's what he always told himself. He didn't have to think about getting through the next year. Not the next six months. Not even the next month or the next week. But he just gave himself thirty minutes at a time.

His method had worked for the past three years, and Levi hoped it would continue to work now.

CHAPTER SIX

"ARE YOU SURE SHE'S DEAD?"

Bobby nodded as he sat in the stiff chair—one that was no doubt designed to make people uncomfortable. That was the way his boss liked it.

"There's no way Dani could have survived the gunshot and the fall into the ocean, especially not with that storm last night. The problem has been taken care of."

"Very well." The man across from him nodded. "Now we should be able to proceed with the rest of our plan."

Bobby ran a hand through his hair, not liking the sound of that. "I just wish there was another way to end this. I didn't realize—"

"This is no time for regrets! Nor is it a time to be sloppy." His boss—the Captain—cast him a warning glare. "We've got to move on this now or we'll lose everything."

Bobby's hands clamped in front of him as he tried to understand what the man was saying. Did his boss think he'd messed up? Bobby had just told the Captain that he'd done exactly what he'd been asked to do.

"Things got out of control. But I handled them."

"What about Paul?"

Bobby's throat tightened. "He stepped out of line. If he hadn't stabbed me in the back—"

"Just listen to yourself," the Captain hissed. "All I hear is excuses."

"Things didn't stay on plan," Bobby's voice trembled. "But I improvised. And I improvised well."

The Captain stared at him, not bothering to hide his scrutiny. Finally, he spoke. "I want you to go to Cape Corral. I need you to confirm Dani is dead."

Bobby sucked in a quick breath. This was a twist he hadn't seen coming. "How am I supposed to do that? Her body was washed out to sea."

"Figure out a way."

There were so many things that could go wrong with that plan. "What if people see me looking around? If I find her body, they're going to think I'm responsible. I'll stick out."

"You are responsible! That's why you need to be the one to make sure this mess is cleaned up." The Captain rose, his tall figure towering and imposing —something else he used to his advantage.

Tension pounded at Bobby's temples. How could this have turned into such a disaster? Now there were dead bodies to take care of. This wasn't what he'd been hired to do. But there was no going back now. He was in too deep.

The Captain stepped closer. "Can I trust you with this? Or are you going to let me down again?"

Bobby raised his chin. He'd already let so many people down. More than anything, he wanted his boss to know how loyal he was. He thought when he'd shot Dani that he'd proven it.

But apparently not.

Now he needed to see it through to completion, to prove that he was worthy to be a part of this plan.

But as his thoughts turned to Dani, his heart panged with grief. He couldn't forget the look of fear in her eyes right before he'd pulled the trigger. He'd never forget that image—or the regret he felt.

"Bobby?" The Captain paced behind him, just out of sight.

His thoughts snapped back to the present, and he nodded. "I'll take care of it. I won't let you down."

His boss clamped his hand down on Bobby's

shoulder. "That's what I was hoping you would say. Now there's no time to waste. I'll have Stewart drop you off."

Bobby nodded and braced himself for what was going to either make or break his career.

And for what could mean life or death for the most important person in his life.

CHAPTER SEVEN

THREE HOURS LATER, a nurse had helped Dani take a shower and clean herself up. Washing her long dark hair and getting all the sand off had felt wonderful. Though her entire body was still sore from everything that had happened, she was grateful to be alive.

The clinic provided some old black yoga pants and a sweatshirt, as well as some flip-flops. The attire wasn't flattering, but it was going to have to work. Thankfully, Dani wasn't trying to impress anybody. Right now, survival was her only concern.

She stared in the bathroom mirror and frowned at the bruise on her cheek. What had happened to her?

She touched the gold chain around her neck. The word "Dani" was written in script on a pendant there. The only clue of who she was.

Dani.

Why didn't it seem familiar to her?

"You okay in there?" someone called from the other side.

The nurse.

Dani sucked in a breath, trying to compose herself. Then she stepped back into her room at the clinic.

After signing some papers and being given some medications, as well as pages of instructions, it was time to leave.

Her life right now almost felt surreal. The fact that she was here at the clinic. The fact that she was being released. The fact that she really didn't even know where she was going.

How was all this possible? Even more . . . how many times could Dani ask herself that question?

She didn't know.

"Are you ready?" the nurse asked as she waited by the door with a wheelchair.

After a moment of hesitation, Dani nodded. "As ready as I'll ever be."

She felt almost shy as the nurse pushed her into the hallway. Levi stood to greet her from a chair that had been set up outside the room. Based on what she'd overheard, the waiting room had been overtaken with a vacationing family that had some sort of stomach bug.

She flashed a quick, uncertain smile at Levi.

Was she shy?

It seemed strange that she even had to ask herself that question. But she wasn't sure. Was it possible to not only forget the details of her life but also to forget the fabric of her being?

"My friend is pulling his SUV up," Levi explained as he fell into step beside them.

"Great." A new kind of tremble rushed through Dani.

Not only could she not remember anything. But now she was also getting a ride with a perfect stranger to a place she wasn't familiar with.

What a nightmare. Maybe this was a terrible idea.

But maybe it wasn't. Besides, Dani didn't have many options. Soon, someone would realize she was gone and come to pick her up. This crazy mess would make sense.

Except for the bullet wound. Would that ever make sense?

Levi walked quietly beside her as the nurse wheeled Dani to an exit. A black SUV waited there, and Levi helped her into the backseat before shutting the door. He then climbed in the front passenger seat, and they took off down the road.

"I'm Grant," the man in the driver's seat said. "Levi and I work together as part of a special commission for Cape Corral's Wildlife Law Enforcement Division."

"Thank you for the ride, Grant." Her voice sounded raw as she said the words.

The man reminded her of Levi, only his gaze seemed more open and his mannerisms more outgoing. Levi seemed serious and reserved.

They were both dressed in a similar manner.

Like cowboys.

Dani still couldn't figure that one out, but now wasn't the time to ask questions.

She had just taken a dose of pain medication, and her eyelids were already getting droopy.

"It's going to take us about twenty minutes to get to the other side of the island," Grant said. "You might as well make yourself comfortable."

"If you need to rest, neither of us will blame you," Levi added.

Dani nodded. Some rest sounded good. There was no good reason to fight it.

She let her head fall against the window beside her as she stared at the landscape.

If only she would wake up to find all of this was just a bad dream. But that was only wishful thinking.

She was going to need all her strength in the coming days if she wanted to heal from her injury and recover the memories of who she was.

Dani wasn't sure she was going to like the picture that emerged.

And that wasn't a great feeling.

"MAYBE WE SHOULD PUT out a press release." Grant kept his voice low as he turned toward Levi. "See if anybody can identify her."

Levi glanced into the backseat. Dani appeared to be sleeping. Her chest rose and fell, and her eyes were closed as her head rested against the window.

Trauma could do that to a person. She might sleep for days, and that slumber might be exactly what her body needed to heal. Resting could be therapeutic.

It had been for him.

"I don't think a press release is a good idea." Levi turned back to Grant, the weight of the situation pressing on him.

"Why not?"

He lowered his voice. "Because someone shot her. My guess is that this person left her for dead. If the gunman knows Dani is still alive . . ."

Grant nodded slowly as Levi's theory hung in the air like a bad premonition. "Good point. Never thought about it that way. You don't think the media is going to get hold of this?"

"As far as they know, a woman washed up on shore. They could have heard that on the scanner, along with the fact that she was rushed to the clinic. I think we should keep the rest under wraps for as long as we can."

"You really think so?" Grant's voice jolted with surprise.

"I do." Levi turned his gaze out the window at the sunny autumn day. "Something about all of this isn't sitting right with me. If we make the wrong move, Dani could end up paying for that with her life."

Grant frowned, his hands gripping the steering wheel as they bounced down the road. "I don't like the sound of that."

"Me either. I don't think we should spread the news all over the island—not until we know more."

"I guess it could go both ways—we talk about her and get answers, or we don't talk about her and keep her safe."

Levi remembered just how helpless the woman had seemed back at the clinic. "My vote is for keeping her safe."

"Understood," Grant said. "When we get back, I'll run her prints. I'll also do a search for any missing women with the first name of Dani or Danielle. Maybe we'll get some hits."

"That sounds good. I did a preliminary search already."

"Did anything pop up?"

Levi shook his head. "No, it didn't. But I want to be prepared in case she doesn't remember for an extended amount of time."

"It could take a few days for someone to report

it. She could have told people she was going on a trip, and maybe they haven't noticed she's not back yet."

Levi chewed on the idea. "It's a possibility. Let's take each day as it comes. We can't afford any wrong moves."

"Good idea. We're lucky to have you around here, Levi. This island wouldn't be the same without you."

Guilt pounded at him. Did Grant know Levi had been offered a position in another town? He'd kept the job offer on the downlow. But that didn't mean that word hadn't somehow leaked. Small towns were notorious for that.

As they continued down the road, Levi's mind continued to race.

He knew he should step back his concern about Dani. He would help the woman by investigating what had happened to her as well as giving her a place to stay. That should be the end of it.

But Levi couldn't stop thinking about finding her on the beach. She'd seemed like a rag doll that had been tossed out to sea before getting spit up by the ocean. Someone had left her for dead.

It wasn't something he could easily forget.

They continued to bump along the street. There were no paved roads on the rest of the island, and residents and visitors needed a four-wheel-drive vehicle to get around. Many people didn't know that before coming, despite the protocols that had been put in place.

That made Lloyd's Towing a very popular business, especially in the summer months when visitors flocked to the area. Lloyd probably towed eight cars each day from the soft sand along the ocean. At least, he had before the washed-out bridge shut things down.

People were fascinated by the area, and Levi couldn't blame them.

Finally, Grant pulled up to Emmy's place, which was located beside the Community Safety Headquarters, a building that housed Fire and Rescue as well as the forestry division that Levi oversaw.

It was time to wake Dani. Levi prayed she'd have as much peace as possible during the coming days.

Because the future would probably be tough on both of them.

Dani, as she recovered.

And Levi, as he tried to figure out who had done this to her.

CHAPTER EIGHT

"HEY, WE'RE HERE." Someone nudged her.

Dani's eyes flew open. In an instant, she jolted back, pressing herself into her seat. Wishing she could disappear. Feeling a terror that was strangely familiar.

Fear captured her breath, her muscles, her thoughts.

Where was she?

Even more—*who* was she?

An ache formed in her heart at the thought.

Slowly, Levi Sutherland's face came into view. His gaze was soft, as if he silently tried to reassure her. He stood beside her open door, and a rustic, sandy landscape showed on the other side.

"It's okay," he murmured. "It's just me. And Grant. We're here. At the inn my sister runs."

That was right. Officer Sutherland—Levi—had

given her a ride from the clinic. Offered her a place to stay.

She could trust him.

Dani thought so, at least.

With so many missing details of her life, it was hard to know whom to rely on. She didn't even know if she could trust herself.

Her lungs loosened for just a moment as Dani glanced around. An old, weathered two-story building sat nearby, sand dunes nestled at the edges. A watchtower stood behind the structure as well as a large garage and another building.

She was okay. She was safe here. At least for a little while. She had no choice but to believe that, especially if she wanted to keep her sanity.

"We just pulled up," Levi said. "Your body needs rest after what you've been through. You slept the entire way here."

Dani tugged at the sweatshirt around her neck. For some reason, the oversized piece of clothing made her feel a small measure of comfort.

"I can show you where you will be staying tonight," Levi said.

"In the meantime, I'm going to check on the horses," Grant added. "I'll catch up with the two of you later."

"Sounds good. Thanks for the ride."

Dani's lungs tightened again. As she stepped

out of the SUV, she felt herself wobble. Levi caught her elbow and helped to steady her.

"I've got you," he murmured.

Dani's cheeks heated—a reaction that made no sense. The man was just doing his job. Yet his quiet reassurance made her feel an unusual peace.

Gathering herself, she walked with Levi toward the house. He kept a hand on her, as if he sensed how off-balance she felt. She was grateful for the support.

She couldn't help but notice the sand beneath her feet. Where was the driveway?

Dani quickly scanned her surroundings. Everywhere she looked, contoured sand stretched over the ground. Even the buildings—several houses and a larger, official looking structure—seemed to be built between dunes.

What kind of place was this? Dani had never seen anything like it.

Then again, maybe this was the perfect location for her. The island seemed so secluded and surreal. Maybe she could heal here while she put the pieces of her life back together—and quickly, at that.

"Right this way." Levi led her into the old house. "My sister converted this place into the island's one and only bed and breakfast."

"That's nice."

"Emmy's not here right now, but she'll be back

soon," Levi continued. "She told me which room you could use."

He led Dani up a set of stairs and to the end of the hallway. The bedroom contained a small bed with an iron headboard and a dresser that had been painted robin's egg blue. It wasn't fancy, but it was clean and neat with a charm of its own.

"I think you'll be comfortable," Levi said. "You're the only one staying here right now, so you'll have some privacy."

"Thank you. I really appreciate this." Dani's throat tightened as she thought about all the unknowns she faced. What she wouldn't do just to have something familiar. But there was no need to wish for the impossible.

"Emmy is going to bring some clothes for you, along with some toiletries. She should be back soon. I know it's not much, but we'll make sure you're taken care of."

Dani pushed her hair behind her ears as she felt a smile flutter across her face. Why was this man having this effect on her? He was like one of those heroes who rode in to save the day in an old cowboy movie.

But too many unknowns haunted her. She needed to remember that and not get too attached. Soon, she'd be returning home. Cape Corral would simply be a blip on the horizon of her life.

Dani cleared her throat as she looked up at

Levi. Her cheeks warmed as she soaked in his handsome features—and then quickly put them out of her mind. "Thank you for everything. I don't know what I would do if I hadn't crossed paths with you."

Levi nodded, the action stiff but friendly. "It's my job."

Her cheeks heated. "Of course. I wasn't trying to imply anything else—"

He raised his hand to halt her thoughts. "No explanation. I know."

Relief rushed through her, and she offered a quick smile, thankful that he understood.

"It's getting late," Levi said. "I'm sure you want to rest. Tomorrow, I'll take you back to the place where you washed ashore, the area where I found you. Maybe you'll remember something."

A ball of ice formed in Dani's chest at Levi's words. Did she really want to see it? Did she want to remember?

She couldn't be sure.

But Dani had no choice but to push ahead.

Not if she wanted answers and if she wanted the person who'd done this to her brought to justice.

LEVI STEPPED onto the sprawling front porch of the inn. He'd wait here until his sister arrived. It wouldn't be smart to leave Dani alone—not until he knew more about the circumstances surrounding her injuries.

He took a deep breath of thick, humid air. The moisture filled his lungs and reminded him why he was ready for cooler weather.

Then again, if Levi took that job up in Maine, he'd always have cooler weather.

At times, the idea was tempting. But things were unsettled in Cape Corral right now. He couldn't make a decision like that in the middle of this turmoil. It was a good thing he'd been given a week.

Today's turn of events left him feeling uneasy. He didn't know what was going on with Dani, but he knew the circumstances appeared dangerous.

That came with the territory when someone with a gunshot wound showed up. What exactly had happened to the woman?

With Dani's sweet disposition, Levi had a hard time seeing her mixed up in something illegal. But that didn't mean she wasn't.

The better possibility was that she'd been a victim. Was this a case of a jealous spouse or boyfriend? A job-related crime? Had she been in the wrong place at the wrong time? All those things were possibilities.

Levi had a lot of work to do if he was going to get to the bottom of this.

Grant appeared from around the corner of the Community Safety building. He wrapped a rope between his elbow and thumb as he paused in front of Levi. "Horses are all doing great."

"That's good news, at least."

"Is Dani settling in?"

"She is. She looked tired so I'm giving her some space. Emmy will check on her when she gets back soon."

"That woman's got a rough road ahead if she doesn't start remembering some of the brouhaha of what happened to her."

"She has a rough road however she looks at it," Levi said. "We've got to find some answers for her."

Just then, an oversized pickup stopped in front of the fire station. Levi's stomach clenched when he saw the driver. Then again, he'd known before the window lowered who was in the overpriced vehicle.

Johnny Ferguson. Thirty years old. The man had never worked a day in his life, and he lived on Cape Corral mostly to flex his social status.

The man thought he and his family owned this island. But they didn't. All the money in the world would never change that.

"Hey, there's a vague scent of manure near my house." Johnny poked his head out the window.

"Any chance someone could come by and clean it up?"

"You're going to have to do that yourself." Levi kept his voice level. The man wasn't going to get a rise out of him.

"I thought that's why we paid you." Johnny smirked as he stared at Levi.

The two didn't get along—especially after Levi had befriended him, only to realize later that Johnny was using him for information. Never again.

Levi stared back at the man, wishing he could wipe the smirk off Johnny's face. "Given the fact you do nothing here on this island, maybe you should make yourself useful."

Johnny's eyes narrowed. "It's my family's tax revenue that funds most of the operations in this place. Need I remind you of that oft-forgotten fact? Without us, there would be no services here."

The Fergusons liked to remind everyone of that detail as often as they could.

"We survived here long before your family ever moved into town," Levi reminded him, keeping his steely gaze on the man.

Johnny let out a grunt before running a hand through his gelled blond hair. "I'd watch yourself, if I were you."

"Is that a threat?" Levi bristled.

"Of course not, officer." He flashed another grin

and tugged at the collar of his crisp linen shirt. "Have a great day."

As Levi watched the man pull away, anger churned inside him. Ever since the Fergusons had moved to the island twelve years ago, the family had been nothing but trouble, had caused nothing but conflict.

And there was no sign of that getting any better.

They were one more reason why leaving this island might be a good thing.

CHAPTER NINE

DANI WAS EXHAUSTED—EXHAUSTED like she'd never known before.

Officer Sutherland had said she could find some water and snacks downstairs. Maybe she should get a quick drink before settling down. So much was on her mind, yet the holes in her memory consumed every thought. The combination didn't mix and left her feeling off balance.

Just as she opened the door to her bedroom to head downstairs, a figure appeared.

Dani gasped and jumped back.

Was it the man who'd shot her? Had he come back to finish what he started?

Her heart thumped in her ears.

Until she realized it was a woman.

With a clothes basket in her hands and an apologetic smile on her face.

"I'm so sorry! I didn't mean to scare you. I was just going to leave a few things outside your door."

Dani glanced at the basket and saw some clothes inside, as well as a toothbrush, toothpaste, and shampoo.

"I'm Emmy Sutherland," the woman said. "I'm Levi's sister, and I run this inn."

Things began to make a little more sense—although Levi and Emmy didn't look that much alike. Emmy had straight, dark hair that came below her shoulders, a trim build, and an easy smile. Levi was lean with light-brown hair and a steely expression.

She remembered her manners.

"I'm Dani—" She paused, feeling that awkward gap where she should say her last name. If only she knew what that last name was.

"I understand that you're having some memory issues." Emmy shifted and moved the basket to her slim hip. "But don't you worry. We'll take real good care of you here. It's kind of what we do."

Dani crossed her uninjured arm over her chest, feeling unreasonably cold. It wasn't because of Emmy. The woman was perfectly warm and hospitable.

The situation in general hit Dani at her core. "Thank you. I appreciate you putting this together for me."

Emmy nodded toward the sling across Dani's

arm and shoulder. "Let me just put it on your bed for you."

Dani stepped aside to let Emmy do that and watched as the woman hustled back to the doorway, almost as if afraid to overdo her welcome.

"Are you heading downstairs?" Emmy nodded toward the staircase.

"I was going to grab some water."

"I'll walk down with you and give you a quick tour of the place."

Emmy's voice lilted with a carefree sound that Dani instantly envied. She didn't fault the woman for it. She only wished she could experience a touch of it.

"That sounds perfect," Dani finally said.

Carefully, she followed Emmy down the wooden staircase of the farmhouse. Shiplap stretched across the walls, and the furniture looked distressed. It was enough to make Chip and Joanna Gaines proud.

Chip and Joanna Gaines? How did Dani remember them and not her own last name?

"This is your place, huh?" Dani asked.

Emmy seemed entirely too young to own a business like this. She seemed more like the type who'd be at a college sorority.

"The house was my grandpa's," Emmy explained, pausing in the living room. "When he passed away two years ago, he left it to me. I decided to open the inn about six months later, in his memory."

"That's great . . . I mean, not your granddad but—"

"I understand." Emmy waved her off, no offense on her face. Then she glanced around. "I like it here. Plus, this place is right next to the Community Safety Building. Since I volunteer with them, it's pretty handy to be so close."

So much about this town made Dani curious. Hopefully, she wouldn't be here long enough to find all the answers. She prayed that, maybe after a good night's sleep, she'd wake up and her memories would be restored.

But she knew that was probably wishful thinking. Dr. Knightly had warned her as much.

Emmy swept her hand in front of her. "Back to my tour. This over here is the dining room. If you keep going down this hall, the kitchen is on your left and a living room on the right. My room is on the other side of the kitchen. Oh, and pay no attention to the graveyard in the backyard."

Dani felt the blood drain from her face. Had she heard that correctly? "The graveyard?"

Emmy paused and flashed a smile, as if she'd been expecting that reaction. "It's an island thing. Actually, when this place was built, nobody knew there was a graveyard. But the sands on the island shift around all the time. Probably about eight years ago, during a particularly big nor'easter, the sand shifted some more, and what do you know? There was a graveyard right in the backyard."

"That's ... fascinating."

"Isn't it? The dates go back into the 1800s, and some seafaring captains are listed on those tombstones. I say it gives the place character." She shrugged nonchalantly. "I mean, if you don't mind graveyards."

"As far as I know I don't mind them." The words sounded strange as they left Dani's lips.

"Interestingly enough, we weren't the only ones this happened to," Emmy continued. "Several homes on the island have graveyards on the property. Some of them even have them in their front yard. That's what happens when you live in a place where the land constantly moves. I suppose there's a Bible verse about that, right? Something about not building your house on shifting sands. There's a lot of wisdom in that. However, there's no place I'd rather be than here in Cape Corral."

Dani smiled at the woman's animated voice. Dani hoped she loved where she lived—wherever that was—equally as much. "I can tell you love it."

Emmy stepped into the kitchen and grabbed a water bottle, handing it to Dani. "I do. And if you stay here long enough, you'll love it too."

Dani didn't remember much about herself, but she had a hard time seeing that. In her gut, she didn't think she was a beach type of girl. She felt more like she lived in the suburbs or on the outskirts of a town.

It was strange how she couldn't remember, but her intuition still tried to tell her things.

"Plus, my brother is here and all my friends," Emmy continued. "Home is where the heart is. That's what they say."

A moment of envy shot through her. Dani wanted a place to feel at home.

When would someone show up looking for her? Offering details that she desperately needed?

Soon, she hoped.

"Can I fix you a sandwich?" Emmy's voice pulled her from her thoughts. "Or I have some leftover pork barbecue that I made at the firehouse last night. The guys said it was pretty good and asked me to make it again, and they're a tough audience."

Despite everything that had happened, Dani found herself smiling. "A sandwich sounds nice. But please don't go out of your way for me. I can certainly manage to make one for myself if you're generous enough to let me eat your food."

Emmy waved her hand in the air. "Oh, it's no problem. I was going to hang out here for a little while anyway. Why don't you have a seat? You've been through a lot."

Dani took a seat on the bench tucked under the

kitchen table. She glanced around again, noticing the wildflower bouquet in a mason jar at the center of the table, the basket of whelk shells, and the glass vase full of sea glass. Emmy had done a great job making this place look inviting.

"Will there be any other guests staying here?" Dani couldn't help but notice how quiet the house felt.

Emmy pulled a few items from the fridge. "I just had someone leave this morning, and I have somebody else coming this weekend. But tonight, it's just you. And, of course, I'll be here."

Dani leaned against the table. "I'd think it would be intimidating running this place all by yourself. I'm assuming you're not married. I don't see a ring."

"Nope, not married." Emmy grabbed some bread. "I probably won't ever get married."

"Why's that?"

Emmy shrugged as she began making a sandwich. "Why would you want to get married when you can be single and roam free—kind of like the horses here? Their only boundaries are nature and loyalty. Isn't that the ultimate way to live?"

"That's one way to look at it." It didn't seem like something Dani would think—not that she could be sure.

"I can do what I want, when I want, how I want right now. I mean, with the exception of my brother and my father, who are constantly telling me what to do." Emmy offered a half eyeroll.

Dani smiled. She didn't even know Emmy that well, but she already liked the woman. She had a plain way of speaking, an easygoing disposition, and the cadence of her words made her seem like everyone's best friend.

Right now, Dani was just thankful that she had a place to stay.

Tomorrow, she'd try to figure out the rest of her future.

She didn't have any other choice.

AFTER LEVI LEFT Dani at the bed and breakfast, he filled out some paperwork regarding Dani's rescue. He also checked news reports for any missing persons fitting Dani's description. He saw nothing, but it would be an ongoing process.

In the meantime, he walked over to the Screen Porch Café for a late lunch/early dinner.

It was the only restaurant on the island, and the establishment looked just like it sounded. Minnie and Mark Minnows lived in the house, but they opened their screened porch to the community. The long-married couple acted as cooks and servers for all their delightful homemade recipes.

The menu was limited and often changed. But

it was a good place to go to grab a bite to eat if someone didn't feel like cooking.

It was also a good place to find out all the local gab.

Which was exactly what Levi wanted to do right now.

He stepped inside, his boots clicking against the bright-blue wood floor. Immediately, the scent of Old Bay and fresh crab meat wafted around him. Several people looked up and called hello.

Minnie emerged from the door with a tray in her hand. "Officer Sutherland. Have a seat. I've got some of my twelve-layer cake ready for you today."

Minnie was like an adopted grandmother to everyone in the area. If someone was sick, she brought them soup. If someone had a baby, she brought a quilt and a pie. Minnie was the first one to volunteer to bring meals to funerals, to make flower arrangements for weddings, or to tell someone they needed to wash behind their ears before potatoes grew there.

There was really everything to love about the woman—and her famous twelve-layer cake.

Levi found a seat at one of the mismatched tables. He chose one against the edge of the oversized screened porch, a place where he could see everybody who came and went.

After Minnie delivered the food to another table, she paced toward him and pulled out her pad and pen. "Officer Levi 'the most handsome law enforcement officer I've ever set my green eyes on' Sutherland. What can I get you, cowboy?"

"Don't you get Mark mad at me, Mrs. Minnie."

The seventy-something's ample hips jutted out, and her gray hair was styled in a neat, poofy halo around her head. But most people noticed her smile first. The grin was big, bright, and consumed her entire face.

Levi glanced at the menu, which had been written on a chalkboard screwed to the outside wall. Every day, Minnie wrote the day's dishes there in almost illegible handwriting.

She didn't care, which made the menu even more endearing.

"I'll take the Lumphrey Bogart," Levi said.

The lump crab cake was served on homemade bread with a rémoulade sauce. It was hands down one of the best crab cakes in the Outer Banks, and Levi had tasted almost all of them. Still, this place was Cape Corral's secret spot, and locals didn't want too many people to discover it. Once Minnie ran out of crab meat, she stopped making the specialty until she got more from local fishermen.

"One Lumphrey Bogart coming right up." Minnie paused and pointed a finger as if conspiring. "And just for you, I'll get an extra-large glass of my sweet tea."

Levi flashed a smile. "That sounds fantastic, Mrs. Minnie. Thank you."

She winked. "It's no problem, cowboy."

As she walked away, Levi glanced around and saw several regulars in the restaurant. He strolled over to a table full of women from church. Fortunately, they were a great source of information here on the island—for better or worse.

"How are you ladies doing today?" Levi paused beside them, tipping his hat their way.

"Just fine, Officer Sutherland." One of the ladies rapidly blinked her eyes as she smiled up at him.

Mary Lou Berkley.

She'd only lived on the island for a couple of years, and she helped with housekeeping at some of the rental houses. She also volunteered to be one of their Sanctuary Watchers.

Watchers made notes and observations about the horses so officials on the island could track the animals. Levi had a feeling Mary Lou had only signed up to help because of him. He didn't mean to sound arrogant, and he'd never say the words aloud. It was simply his impression of the woman.

Every time Mary Lou volunteered, she tracked down Levi—and only Levi—to share her findings. The guys at the station had taken to giving him a hard time about it.

"Anything new out there today?" Levi asked.

Mary Lou blinked some more, her thick mascara—and glimmering eyeshadow—looking unnatural on her eyes. The woman looked more "big city" than she did untamed island. Somehow, she managed to use enough hairspray to keep her blonde hair in place, despite the island's constant wind and humidity.

"I looked for Skeeter today." Mary Lou twirled her lemonade with a paper straw. "I didn't see him with his mama."

Levi's back muscles pinched at her words. "It's unusual for a foal to separate from his mom."

"I only saw his mom, Cookie, for a moment and then she went trotting into the woods." Mary Lou shrugged. "Too many ticks out there for me to follow."

"Not that we want you following the horses anyway," Levi reminded her.

She nodded, maybe a little too quickly. "Of course. Anyway, I was just hoping to catch a glimpse of the little guy. Too bad I didn't."

Levi didn't like the sound of that.

If Skeeter wasn't with his mom then the foal could be in trouble.

It was one more thing Levi needed to add to his list of things to do today.

CHAPTER TEN

"ALL THE OTHER HORSES APPEAR OKAY?" Levi glanced around the table.

Each person there nodded. Every local—every true local—thought of themselves as an unofficial guardian of this place and the creatures inhabiting it.

That was good news, at least.

"Actually, Officer Sutherland, I was hoping I might run into you. Could I have a word?" Kayla Peters, their island realtor, glanced up at him, waiting for his response.

"Of course."

They stepped outside and padded across the soft sand, away from any listening ears, before Kayla spoke. Still, Kayla glanced around as if to make sure no one was listening.

"I know this is none of my business," she

started. "But I just thought I'd let you know that I got another offer today on that land out in the North Banks."

Levi's hands went to his hips. Levi knew Kayla liked to look out for the island just as much as he did. He appreciated her loyalty.

"Who put in the offer?" he asked.

Kayla frowned, flipping a honey-blonde hair from her eyes. "It's a corporation. This is the fourth lot they've put an offer on in the past several months."

Levi didn't like the sound of that. "Did this corporation state their intentions?"

Her shoulders looked like they clenched with tension. "The property is zoned for residential, of course. But, as you and I both know, it would be a shame to lose that land to more development. The landscape of this island is just going to keep changing unless we put a stop to it."

"As long as the county officials keep making the decisions that they do, it's going to be hard to stop it." Levi shifted, still absorbing the new information. "Whose name is on the lease? Can you tell me that?"

She shrugged and glanced around again. "I wish I could. Like I said, it's a corporation—Wilhelmina Incorporated, whatever that is. We've been doing everything via email. In fact, we don't even have to meet face-to-face to do a closing anymore. It's a blessing and a curse."

"I don't like the sound of this." Levi rubbed his jaw, reminding himself not to grit his teeth as he was prone to do when stressed—and this day was definitely starting to feel stressful.

"I don't either. The good news is that the property is pretty much landlocked. Ed Wilkes owns the lot in front of it. In order to get to the property, he'd have to approve an easement through his land."

"That is good news," Levi told Kayla. "Thank you for letting me know. If you hear anything else, will you tell me?"

"Of course."

Just as Levi stepped back inside, Minnie came out with his sandwich.

Good. He was hungrier than he'd thought. He'd missed lunch because he'd been at the clinic, and it was almost past dinnertime now.

As Levi took the first bite, the crisp but fresh flavor of the crab cake washed over his taste buds. He could die a happy man if he was eating one of these sandwiches when he went.

Only halfway through the meal, thunder rumbled in the distance.

Was there another storm coming?

Levi had a feeling there was—and he wasn't just talking about a physical storm. No, he could feel things stirring up on the island, and he didn't like it.

And somehow, all of this turbulence just might go back to the island's newest visitor—Dani.

Levi needed to get to the bottom of who she was and what she was doing here.

CHAPTER ELEVEN

BOBBY STOOD atop the sand dune and looked around.

Stewart had dropped him off at a dock on the west side of the island. An old house was nestled behind some nearby woods, secluded from the rest of the community. Bobby could stay overnight without being noticed.

Right now, he had to concentrate on Dani.

Bobby's heart panged with another moment of regret as he thought about her. He wished she hadn't gotten caught in the middle of this. But he couldn't go back now. What was done was done.

Despite what the Captain said, Bobby knew there was no way Dani could have survived what happened. She'd been shot and had fallen into the ocean. If the bullet hadn't killed her, then the treacherous sea would have.

He glanced around again, thankful that the darkness concealed him. Bobby needed to figure out a way to cover up his real identity while he was in town. The community was close-knit, and someone like him would stick out like a proverbial sore thumb.

As he glanced in the distance, he saw a storm brewing. An omen of what was to come? Maybe.

He looked farther down the shore, where lights from various homes shone. The community really was quiet. Peaceful. Unlike anything he'd ever seen before.

With that thought in his mind, he knew what he needed to do. He needed a new identity. A cover story. And he had his eyes peeled and his ears open for any news about a dead body that had washed ashore.

As soon as he found that confirmation, he'd go back to the Captain and tell him the update. Job done.

The sooner he got this over with, the better.

Because if anyone would have to take the fall for this, it was Bobby.

And he would pay dearly—or, he should say, his son would.

CHAPTER TWELVE

AFTER FINISHING DINNER, Levi went into the office for a few hours before starting home. He wanted to get there before the storm came, though he predicted the system would remain offshore.

Darkness had fallen. The nighttime was even darker out here in the absence of any streetlights. The only illumination was that glowing from windows of nearby houses and from the moon and the stars overhead.

Despite the storm that paraded across the ocean, the moon still shone. Tonight, it was only a sliver. He could also see the Milky Way stretching across the heavens. The sight was fantastic, something Levi never got tired of.

Since he couldn't pick up his truck from the shop until tomorrow, he decided to walk home. His cottage wasn't far away, and the action would give him time to clear his head.

The sand padded his footsteps, silencing them and giving him space to think—and he had a lot to think about.

Dani and her mysterious—and dramatic—entrance here on the island.

His conversation with Kayla about the Wilhelmina Corporation.

The decision about his job.

The fact that no one had seen their foal, Skeeter, for a couple of days.

Levi was going to have his hands full over the next week.

That familiar feeling of apprehension pinched his muscles. Levi paused and glanced around, trying to locate the source.

His eyes narrowed as he glanced at a house in the distance.

Mr. Henderson's place. A single bulb lit the area near the man's back door, scattering hazy light.

Was that a man crouching outside?

If it was Mr. Henderson, the man would have waved or come over to shoot the breeze for a little while. For hours, most likely.

But this person had darted out of sight.

Caution tugged at Levi.

He circled the house but saw nothing.

Strange.

He'd definitely seen someone out here. But whoever it was appeared to be long gone.

Before Levi could continue home, his radio let out a burst. He lifted it to his ear to hear what was being said.

"Sutherland, it's Matthews. We have problem, something you're going to want to see."

Levi's back muscles stiffened at Grant's grim tone. "What's going on?"

"A dead body was just discovered over here by the North Banks."

Alarm raced through Levi. A dead body?

What exactly was going on here in Cape Corral?

YOU LEFT me with no choice!

Dani jolted upright in bed. Sweat covered her skin, and her heart raced.

Her gaze darted around. She braced herself to see danger hovering nearby.

Instead, her temporary room here at the inn stared back, the darkness barely illuminated by the greenish glow of the small clock beside her bed.

No one else was here. Just her.

She let out a breath.

Her dreams had messed with her head.

What had that nightmare been about? Or was it a memory?

Dani ran a hand through her hair as she tried to control her thoughts—and her pulse.

The voice in her dream had been faceless. Dani didn't know who had said the words.

But they caused terror to rip through her.

Dani rubbed her arms as another shiver raced down her spine.

If only she could remember just a little, like the names of her friends. Someone who could fill in the blanks for her.

But those words from her nightmare kept echoing in her mind as a cold sweat spread across her skin.

You left me with no choice.

Her fingers dug into her quilt. Those almost sounded like words that someone she knew might say.

Right before they pulled the trigger.

She tugged the blanket up around her.

Then a new thought hit. What if Dani had been shot because she was on the wrong side of the law? In her gut, Dani thought she was an innocent victim. But if there was a gun involved . . . what if her role had been criminal?

Nausea churned inside her. She hated feeling so lost.

Officer Sullivan's face flashed in her mind again.

But if she really was a criminal, certainly the man would discover that. In fact, what if Levi stormed over to the inn this morning and arrested Dani for a crime she couldn't remember committing?

She shook her head. Her thoughts bounced all over the place. None of them made sense.

The only thing she knew for certain was the fact her heart raced and sweat covered her skin.

Whatever had happened to her, her subconscious knew about it. Was clinging to it. Was signaling to Dani that it was too traumatic to recall. Instead, the facts had been locked away and the key was gone—for now, at least.

A tear trickled down the side of her face.

What a nightmare.

Dani nestled deeper in her bed, wishing she could somehow escape from this situation unscathed. But she knew that wasn't a possibility.

She also knew that Levi Sutherland was a huge blessing.

As she remembered what a gentleman the man had been, her cheeks warmed.

At once, his image filled her mind. His light-brown hair. His barely there beard and mustache. His trim body, pale blue eyes, and steady gaze.

He seemed like a true cowboy, like the ones

people heard about on TV shows or in one of those books.

How did she remember these things but not remember her last name? Yet, for some reason, she did.

It made no sense.

Thunder rolled again, Mother Nature letting everyone around her know who was in control.

Kind of like Dani's life right now. She was living, but she had no grounding and was at the mercy of her circumstances.

Dani pulled the blanket up around her neck again, craving some sort of comfort.

Maybe somebody would show up tomorrow. Her friends were probably worried sick about her. Maybe they had been searching for her.

And then, maybe they'd tell her who she was and what had happened.

Dani squeezed her eyes shut, praying that was the case.

Because if she had to live like this for a long time, she didn't know how she was going to hold it all together.

CHAPTER THIRTEEN

"WHO DISCOVERED THE BODY?" Levi asked.

His crew was already on the scene, along with members of Fire and Rescue. They'd set up lights on the dunes to illuminate the area.

But what Levi saw was macabre.

A man's face, hands, and knees protruded from the sand.

His lifeless face.

Based on what Levi observed, the man hadn't been dead long. Decomposition hadn't begun yet.

Levi studied the man's face but didn't recognize him.

"Wanda Ferguson called it in." Grant stared down at the victim and frowned. "Apparently, she was taking a walk when she stumbled upon the body. Said she didn't know what she'd run into at first. When she pulled out her phone and turned on the light, she got the surprise of her life."

"I bet she did."

Wanda was Johnny's mother, and she was only slightly more bearable than her son and her husband. Still, Levi didn't wish any harm on her, and certainly a discovery like this would be tough to stomach.

As Levi glanced back, he spotted the woman standing on the edge of the crime scene. Her husband stood beside her, an arm around her shoulders. Someone must have told her she couldn't leave until they got her statement.

Levi turned back toward Grant. "Anything noteworthy that you observed when you got here?"

"Not really. I didn't see any gunshot wounds or unusual bruising. Again, it's dark, and most of his body is covered by sand."

"Keep an eye on the scene until the doc gets here. I need to talk to Mrs. Ferguson."

"Yes, sir."

Levi strode toward Wanda, drawing on every last ounce of his cordiality as he approached. He had to go through the process every time he had an encounter with this family. He couldn't let them think they had any amount of control over him—because they didn't.

"I heard you were the one to find the body," Levi started.

Wanda was in her fifties and thin, with dark hair cut in a sharp bob. She'd aged well—and she knew it. Speculation around town was that she'd gone under the knife more than once.

"I did, and I don't have anything else to say." Wanda frowned and leaned closer to her husband. "I wish you would just let me go home. I'm exhausted and there's a storm off-shore."

"It's going to skirt around us," Levi told her as another rumble of thunder filled the air. "I promise not to take up too much of your time. Now, do you always walk by yourself at this time of night?"

Wanda narrowed her gaze, raising a hand to her chin and displaying fingers adorned with fancy, expensive rings and a wrist covered in gold bracelets. "What are you implying, officer?"

"I'm not implying anything, ma'am. I'm just trying to paint a picture of what happened tonight." He kept his voice professional.

Levi's words seemed to appease her, and she lowered her hand.

For good measure, she harrumphed before continuing. "I'll have you know I decided to walk to the beach. There's nothing illegal about that."

"And as you were walking you just happened to come across this man?" Levi clarified.

"That's right. It was hard to see, but I figured there wasn't anything out here that was dangerous."

"Don't forget cottonmouth snakes. And the wild boars. And an occasional bear." Levi was constantly in the process of educating people about the dangers of island life. Some people never seemed to get it.

Wanda's gaze narrowed. "Anyway, I stumbled on something and thought it was a branch in the sand. But when I shone my light down, imagine my surprise when I saw a face staring back at me." The woman visibly shuddered.

For a moment, Levi actually felt bad for her. The discovery would shock anyone.

"Did you recognize the man?" Levi continued.

Wanda's gaze narrowed even more. "You certainly don't think I'm connected with this, do you?"

"Again, I'm not jumping to any conclusions, ma'am. I'm just gathering evidence."

"I've never seen the man before." Wanda raised her chin as if daring Levi to doubt her.

"And have you seen anything suspicious going on in this area lately?" Levi's mind raced back to Dani.

Did her appearance and this man's death have something to do with one another? Levi would be a fool if he didn't ask himself that question. The timing couldn't be denied.

"No, I haven't. Then again, I just got back into town this morning. I went into Norfolk to do some shopping for the weekend. So if you're thinking I had anything to do with this, you're wrong. I can verify my alibi." Her voice rose with defensiveness.

It didn't seem to matter what Levi told her. Wanda wasn't going to believe him when he said that she wasn't a suspect. Not yet, at least. But he was in Ferguson territory now up here on the northern tip of the island.

The family was secretive, not only about what they did with their time but about how they got their money. They seemed to like to keep people guessing. Even worse, they thought they were above the law. But Levi wasn't about to back down to someone who felt entitled. He'd fought too hard to earn everything he had to give in to that.

"Thank you for your help." Levi tapped his pen against his pad before putting it away. "You're free to go."

He had Wanda's phone number and knew where she lived. If Levi had any follow-up questions, he'd find her.

For now, he wanted to figure out what had happened to this John Doe. Because dead bodies were not an everyday occurrence here on Cape Corral.

AN HOUR LATER, Dr. Knightly stood and wiped the sand from his knees. It had already been a long, long night, and it wasn't going to get shorter anytime soon.

"It looks like blunt force trauma." Dr. Knightly turned to Levi with a frown. "That's not my official opinion. I won't share that until I do an autopsy. But, just from looking at him, that's what appears to have happened."

"Where did this blunt force trauma occur?" Levi asked.

"There's some bruising around his ribs and also on the back of his head."

That didn't sound good. "Any idea what he was hit with?"

The doctor frowned again, and Levi could tell there was something he didn't want to say.

"What is it, Doc?" Levi asked.

"Based on the shape of the bruise, I'm inclined to think he was kicked by . . . a horse."

Levi blanched at his words. "You think a horse did this?"

"I think a horse did *part of this* at least. Obviously, the horse couldn't bury the man in the sand. But if you look at the direction of the wind, my guess is that our John Doe was totally buried and then, as the wind blew and shifted the sand, his body was exposed. I'd put his time of death at last night, probably shortly after midnight."

Levi chewed on his words for a moment.

Grant stepped closer. "What if one of the horses kicked him in the ribs and took him down to his knees? While he was on his knees, maybe the horse kicked the back of his head. It could have been a fatal blow."

That was exactly what Levi had been thinking. But then who had buried him?

"It's a plausible theory," Knightly said.

"Obviously, he wasn't alone," Grant started. "You think this has something to do with that foal we haven't seen?"

The thought had run through Levi's head. "It's a possibility. I'm still not convinced that we won't find Skeeter. There are a lot of places to hide here on this island."

"That's true. But we should probably examine that possibility." Grant lowered his voice. "As should we examine the possibility that this woman we found, Dani, could have had something to do with this also."

As Grant said the words, more lightning flashed offshore and the breeze kicked up.

"A gun hasn't been found in the brush anywhere, has it?" Levi asked.

Grant raised his shoulders. "Not to my knowledge. Of course, we'll keep looking as soon as it's daylight and easier to see."

"What about an ID?" Levi's mind continued to race. "Did you find any on the victim?"

"We didn't," Grant said. "We can run the man's prints through the system, of course."

"Yes, we definitely need to do that."

Something was going on here on this island. Levi wasn't going to rest until he figured out what kind of darkness had invaded his home.

CHAPTER FOURTEEN

LEVI SHOT upright on the sofa as he heard a noise in the distance.

Emmy stood in the living room staring at him. "You slept here?" she muttered. "You said you were just going to relax for a few minutes before heading home last night."

He ran a hand over his face, wishing away his grogginess. "With everything happening here on the island, I didn't think it was a good idea to leave you and Dani alone."

Emmy turned to him, hands on her hips. "I'm sure I'd be fine, but it was probably a good call concerning Dani, since she was shot and all."

Levi ran a hand over his face again, still trying to shake off his sleepiness. He'd been up for most of the night. When he saw his sister's lights still on at three a.m., he'd swung by to make sure everything was okay.

It wasn't long afterward he'd fallen asleep on the couch.

"I guess you haven't heard from our guest yet this morning?" Levi glanced at the stairs as yesterday's events returned to the forefront of his thoughts.

"Not yet." Emmy sat across from him in an oversized chair with a white slipcover. "So, what do you know about Dani?"

It seemed entirely too early to have this conversation, but Levi wasn't sure when they'd have another opportunity. "Not much since she can't remember anything. I'm going to take her to the spot where I found her yesterday. I'm hoping that might trigger something."

"It's a mystery. Very interesting." Emmy laced her hands together in front of her, her eyes brimming with curiosity.

"It's definitely a mystery."

Someone knocked at the front door then stepped inside before Emmy could answer.

Colby Morris, one of the volunteer firefighters on Cape Corral and Emmy's best friend since childhood. The two had been nearly inseparable since they were ten.

The man was the same age as his sister: twenty-four. He had light-blond hair, mischievous blue eyes, and a lean but strong frame.

"Looks like it's already a busy day at the station." Colby paused in front of them. "I heard about all the excitement yesterday—and last night. It's hard to believe this is all happening here in Cape Corral."

Levi was sure by now that most of the island had heard about what was going on. Word spread like wildfire here on this island.

"Any chance I could get some coffee before we talk too much?" Levi asked.

"I'll grab some for you." Emmy stood and disappeared into the kitchen.

"Yesterday definitely wasn't a typical day here," Levi told Colby. "Who's doing the rounds this morning?"

"Grant and Dash headed out, and Acadia went with them. They're looking for KitKat."

Acadia Jeffries was the island's veterinarian. She helped the team monitor the horses and treated them when necessary. One of their horses, KitKat, had been standing in the same spot for the past two days, and Acadia was worried that something may have happened to her.

"There were a few Sanctuary Watcher forms in the mailbox." Colby held up three sheets of paper.

Emmy appeared and handed Levi some coffee with her usual flair. She acted like she'd given him a golden scepter the way she held her hands out to him.

"Thank you," Levi muttered before turning back to Colby. "Did you look at the sheets yet?"

"I glanced through them. Everything looked good."

Just as Colby finished his statement, footsteps sounded on the stairs. A moment later, an uncertain looking Dani appeared. She ran her fingers through the tips of her hair and offered an almost shy smile as she reached the first floor.

"Good morning." She wrapped her arms over her chest—the one in the sling already in that position. "I thought I heard someone down here."

Levi felt his breath catch when he saw her. He wasn't sure why he had the reaction. It wasn't like he'd never seen a beautiful woman before. He'd been married to one, for that matter.

But there was just something so raw and vulnerable about Dani. Those qualities made him want to protect her with everything he had in him. He reminded himself to remain at arm's length and do his job—and nothing more.

"Just in time." Emmy stood and turned to face Dani. "Levi was about to start breakfast."

Levi's eyebrows shot up at his sister's words. "I was?"

"I've been craving your French toast with

caramel sauce and bananas. Please say you'll make it."

He glanced at his watch, considering his options. "I've got an hour."

"Perfect. I'll pull the ingredients out and also the griddle." Emmy turned on her heel and headed toward the kitchen. "Colby, you have just enough time to fix my leaking sink!"

"On it!" He rose to his feet.

Dani pointed at Emmy's fleeing figure. "I'll help in the kitchen. It's the least I can do."

"I'm sure no one will mind if you rest," Levi told her. "You've been through a lot."

"I want to stay busy. It helps me keep my mind off things."

He frowned. "No memories?"

"No memories." Dani frowned and pointed to Emmy. "I think I will help, if you don't mind. Talking to you right now has reminded me that nothing has changed. I'd rather forget that."

"Of course." Levi understood her urge to keep her thoughts occupied.

He couldn't blame her.

As she disappeared into the kitchen, Levi's gaze trailed her.

He had a feeling that whatever was going on with Dani was far from being over. But Levi hoped his gut was wrong. He hoped Dani remembered her name and details about her life and that she'd be able to continue on her merry way.

However, he had a feeling that wouldn't be happening.

DANI REMAINED QUIET DURING BREAKFAST. The French toast was delicious, especially with the fresh whipped cream and caramel. Emmy had been right—Dani would definitely be craving more of this dish.

Having food in her stomach felt good, as did listening to the banter around her. Dani had so much to figure out about this new place where she was staying.

All she knew right now was that this was an island with an old inn, cemeteries in the backyard, and cowboys.

It almost seemed like Dani was in a whole different world—though she couldn't know that for sure. She wasn't sure if she was frightened by this place or fascinated. Under ordinary circumstances, she'd definitely say fascinated.

After they finished eating, Colby offered to clean up, betting he could get it all done before the song "Should've Been a Cowboy" could finish playing on his phone.

As the strands of the song drifted across the

room, Levi turned to Dani. "Are you ready to go to the beach? To see if it triggers any memories?"

Dani wasn't sure if she really wanted to remember, but she nodded anyway. "That sounds good."

"All right then." He stepped toward the door, lightly placing his hand on her back. "Let's get going."

They stepped into the bright morning sunlight that flooded the porch. The storm had bypassed them and the air was already heavy with humidity, but the sky was blue and promising.

Dani sucked in a deep breath, grateful for the fresh air—no matter how thick it might be. Despite her circumstances, she still had so much to be grateful for.

Levi paused in front of her. "Do you like horses?"

"I . . . I don't know." Dani had no idea where he was going with this.

He let out a self-reprimanding chuckle. "I guess you don't. Sorry."

"No, it's okay. It takes some getting used to, doesn't it? I wish I knew what I liked and what I didn't."

"I can only imagine." He paused before continuing. "I usually patrol the area on horseback. It keeps me in tune with the island and the way life here was meant to be. But we'll take one of the

Forestry Division's Jeeps, especially with your injury."

"Whatever is best for you."

"Let me introduce you to Nelly first. I like to check on her every morning."

Dani followed Levi behind the safety headquarters to the stables located at the back of the property. As she stepped inside, the scent of hay drifted around her, trying to sweep her back to another time.

Another time? Had she worked with horses? She wished she knew.

"This building seems out of place here," Dani said. "There's nothing else out here but some homes."

Levi slowed his steps. "Almost nothing on this island was planned—a fact that kind of fits the community. On the south end of the island you'll find the clinic, post office, and a small general store. A little farther up, you'll hit the island's only restaurant—the Screen Porch Café. This building is one of the few that was purposefully built in a chosen location. It's in the middle of the island, making it central in case of any emergencies."

"Sounds smart. What about farther up north?"

"There are still a few original houses, but some bigger vacation homes are also being built there."

"Very interesting."

He offered a quick smile. "I think so too."

Dani spotted two men in the distance. One brushed a horse and the other carried a bucket of water. Dani recognized one of them as Grant, the man who'd been at the hospital yesterday. The other man was thinner and whistled to himself as he brushed one of the eight horses there.

Levi paused by one of the stalls. Then he reached inside and rubbed a chestnut-colored mare on the head. "Dani, this is my horse, Nelly. Nelly, this is Dani."

"Hello, Nelly." She reached forward and let the horse sniff her hand before rubbing the side of her face. "She's beautiful."

"She's one of a kind," Levi said. "We've been inseparable for the past ten years."

"Sounds like quite the bond."

He looked up at the horse and affectionately rubbed her head, his entire disposition softening. "It is."

Dani wondered about the wistfulness in his voice. If she knew Levi better, she might ask. But his personal life was none of her business.

As the horse neighed, Dani's mind swirled.

She squeezed her eyes shut, her mind trying to transport her back in time.

To darkness.

To panic.

To the scent of ocean water.

She gasped. Danger. Whatever was happening, it was dangerous.

One of the horses was frightened. Someone yelled. Dani cowered.

"No!"

"Dani?" A hand came down on her arm.

Her eyes flung open. With labored breathing, her gaze focused on her surroundings.

It wasn't dark. There was no panic.

There was just Levi. The stables. Nelly.

"Did you remember something?" he asked, studying her face.

"It was . . . only a feeling, actually." She rubbed her throat. "I remember feeling scared. Knowing that the situation was dangerous. But no details."

"Just give it time."

She nodded. "I will."

Levi continued to stare at her. "We should probably get going. I just needed to check on Nelly, and I thought you might want to meet her. In my world, horses make everything better."

Dani smiled at his words.

She liked the sound of that.

CHAPTER FIFTEEN

FIFTEEN MINUTES LATER, Levi and Dani headed toward the beach, the Jeep bouncing over the sand.

"So, how long have you lived here?" Dani raked her hand through her hair as the wind whipped through it.

"My entire life, give or take a few years."

"Really? I didn't think people stayed in one place for that long."

He shrugged, not seeming offended by her questions. "I went off to college. Thought I might go into business. But my heart was here in Cape Corral, so I came back."

She glanced at the rugged landscape around her. Something about these windswept shores put her soul at ease, made it easier to breathe. Perhaps it was the reminder that an unseen artist had painted broad strokes over this island and created a place full of imagination and tranquility.

"It's certainly a unique area," Dani finally said.

"It is. Eight thousand acres. We have just as many wild horses as we do full-time residents."

Dani let that fact sink in for a minute. "That's pretty amazing."

"We've been getting more visitors in recent years. A lot are fisherman. Some people just come here for the experience of it or because they want to see the wild horses. It's a mixed blessing, to be honest."

"Why is that?" The island was intriguing, and Dani wanted to learn all she could about it. The more she knew, the better off she figured she would be. It would somehow make her feel more grounded.

"We want to keep things safe for the horses. In order to do that, we need to keep too much of the island from being developed." Levi paused and sucked in a deep breath, the picture of calm and collected. "But for the past decade, there's been somewhat of a war between the two different mindsets here on the island."

"What do you mean?"

"There are people who want to keep this place the way it's always been, and then there are the people who think that the island needs to be developed in order to be prosperous."

Dani studied his steadfast expression. "I take it you're one of the ones who thinks it needs to stay the way it is."

"I want what's best for these horses. The more development, the more chances of accidents. Plus, it doesn't matter how many times we tell visitors not to touch or feed the horses. Inevitably, we catch them doing it all the time. I can't seem to get through to people how that's detrimental to their health."

"I could see where that would be a problem." Dani glanced around as they headed down the sandy street. "This place . . . the roads aren't paved. They're just paths in the sand. Why is that?"

"This place is basically a shifting sandbar. Mother Nature is going to do what Mother Nature wants to do. It wasn't worth the cost of constantly having to repave the streets when one of the sand dunes shifts one direction or another. It was more of a strategic move."

"Well, it certainly is fascinating. I can see why you like it here." Dani meant the words. She'd never been in a place like this before.

A moment later, he braked by the shoreline. Levi climbed out before rushing around to assist Dani. As he took her hand to help her out, a charge of electricity rushed through her.

Electricity? That couldn't be right.

Maybe the man had reached hero status in her

mind. That had to be it. There was no reason she should be feeling this way.

Quickly, she cleared her throat, trying to hide her surprise rush of attraction. Levi didn't seem to notice. Instead, they both stood in silence as they stared at the rolling ocean waves that pounded the shore.

"This is it?" Dani finally asked, her throat burning as the words left her lips.

Levi offered a tight nod. "I found you right here."

Dani glanced around. A wide beach stretched in front of the expansive ocean. Behind her, a sand dune rose to protect the houses behind it.

What in the world happened for her to end up here?

Dani still had no idea.

And she wouldn't stop asking herself those questions until she had answers.

LEVI WATCHED DANI'S EXPRESSION. He saw no signs of recognition flash across her gaze.

Despite that, he still asked, "Anything?"

She pulled her arms across her chest and shook her head. "No, nothing."

Levi bit back his disappointment. He'd known he was wishing for too much, but that hadn't stopped him from hoping that Dani might remember something.

She seemed to sense his disappointment, and her gaze fluttered up to meet his. "I'm sorry."

He gently touched her arm, trying to let her know it was okay. "You have nothing to be sorry about. It's still early. Maybe with some time, things will make more sense."

"Maybe," Dani muttered. But she looked unconvinced as she nibbled on her lip. "What now?"

In practical terms, Levi needed to follow up about the dead man they'd discovered last night. But he didn't believe in coincidences. Finding Dani and then their John Doe? The crimes were most likely connected.

If he was able to stay close to Dani, maybe he could find answers.

Levi pulled out his phone and clicked on a picture of their John Doe. He'd taken it this morning, after Dr. Knightly had cleaned up the corpse some. The picture wasn't overly gruesome, and he thought Dani could handle seeing it.

"Do you recognize this man?" He held his phone up and showed the photo to her.

She stared at the image a moment. As she did, Levi watched her reaction for any sign of recognition or deceit.

He saw neither of those things—only confusion and frustration.

"I don't." Her gaze flashed up to meet his. "Should I?"

Levi put his phone away. "Not necessarily. I just had to ask."

"Who is he? Or should I say, who *was* he?" Dani's voice cracked as she asked the questions, and she rubbed her throat.

"That's what we're trying to figure out. We discovered his body last night."

Her face paled. "You found a dead body? Here?"

"We did." Skirting around the truth wouldn't do either of them any favors.

Levi sensed her knees weakening. He grabbed her elbow and caught her before she sank to the ground. To be safe, he led her to the Jeep and lingered close by as she leaned against the bumper.

"I don't understand . . ." Dani shook her head, as if trying to make pieces fit that she couldn't quite visualize.

"We're still investigating. This is just the beginning."

"What a nightmare." She ran a hand over her face as if she couldn't believe it. What had happened was a lot for anyone to comprehend.

"Hey." Levi bent toward her. "It's going to be okay."

"Nothing feels okay right now."

"I know. But you just have to know that there's hope in sight, okay?"

Her gaze flashed with an unknown emotion as she looked up at him. "You sound like you speak from experience."

At once, images from Levi's past filled his mind. Images of losing Adrienne. Images of the darkness that hovered over him afterward.

But that wasn't something he wanted to talk about right now, especially not with this stranger. Too many other things demanded his attention.

"I do speak from experience," he finally settled on saying. "That's how I know you're going to get through this."

"How?" Dani stared at Levi as if he had all the answers.

If only that was the case.

"You'll figure it out. Just give it some time." Levi squared his shoulders. "For now, I need to make another round here on the island. Then I'll drop you off at the inn so I can continue investigating our victim."

Dani nodded, but Levi knew she was still torn up over everything that had happened.

Maybe seeing more of the island would help cheer her up.

That always worked for him.

At least, it had until after Adrienne.

CHAPTER SIXTEEN

DANI SUCKED in a breath as the wind kissed her face. Something about cresting the dunes and seeing the ocean helped to set her mind at ease.

At least, it did until she remembered everything that was happening. Yet she didn't remember hardly anything—only the uncertainty of her circumstances as well as the fact that it had been twenty-four hours since she'd been found.

As if it wasn't bad enough that she couldn't remember who she was, now Dani couldn't stop thinking about that dead man. What if that man's death was somehow connected with her gunshot wound?

It went back to the question Dani had been asking herself yesterday. What if she *had* been mixed up in something unsavory? She didn't want to believe it was possible, but Dani would be naive if she didn't explore that option.

She shoved the questions aside as Levi pointed out various sites while they rode between the dunes. Wild horses roamed everywhere, including beneath some of the stilted structures. Levi told her that, when the horses got hot, they liked to wander into the shaded areas the houses offered.

The creatures really were beautiful, and Dani could see why people would enjoy themselves here. If only she was in Cape Corral for fun.

But she wasn't—not by any stretch of the imagination.

She cleared her throat. A question had pressed on her all morning, a question she hadn't wanted to voice out loud. But she had to know the truth.

"Has anyone called about me yet?" Her quivering voice made her sound entirely more vulnerable than she'd intended. Dani cleared her throat again, wishing she sounded stronger than she did.

Levi's lips pressed together as his hands gripped the steering wheel. "No, I'm sorry. They haven't."

Despair pressed on her. Was she a loner? Did she have no friends? No one to notice she was missing?

If that was the case, what kind of person had she been? Someone utterly unlovable?

Tears tried to push to her eyes, but Dani held them back.

Levi stole a quick glance at her. "Maybe your family thinks you're on vacation—somewhere without cell service."

Dani supposed that was a possibility. Maybe she'd told people she was going somewhere by herself. Maybe people would only notice she was missing when she failed to return home on time.

At least, Dani would like to believe that's what was going on.

But the truth was, what if she didn't have anybody?

She glanced at her hand. She didn't see any tan lines where a wedding ring might have been at one time. Could she safely assume she was single?

She didn't know that either.

And Dani hated not knowing these things.

What if that man who'd turned up dead had been . . . her husband? Or her boyfriend?

A sick feeling rose in Dani at the thought of it.

Maybe she shouldn't *want* to remember.

Maybe those details were too painful and forgetting them was actually a blessing.

"LISTEN, do you mind if I swing by my place for a minute?" Levi asked.

"Not at all."

"I just need to grab something I forgot this morning."

"Of course."

A few minutes later, Levi pulled to a stop at the small cottage he called home. He'd bought this place after Adrienne died. The house they'd shared together held too many memories, and it had been too painful to stay there without her.

Which was one more reason why Levi might want to leave the island.

He hadn't gone out seeking other jobs. But one of his friends from college was now the mayor in a little town in Maine—and by little, Levi meant a hundred thousand residents.

When the former police chief had retired, Langston had called Levi.

Levi hadn't expected to be tempted by the offer—but he was.

He'd been feeling for a while that he needed a change in his life. Maybe a new town and a new job fit the bill.

He let out a sigh as he returned to the present. He glanced at Dani beside him in the Jeep. The sun was beating down on her, especially since there was no top on the vehicle.

"It's going to get hot out here," he told Dani. "Why don't you come inside a moment?"

She nodded and slipped her seatbelt off.

Together, they climbed the steps to his doorway. He didn't have people over here very often, and it was the ultimate bachelor pad. It was a good thing he wasn't trying to impress anyone.

"Have a seat." Levi pointed to a dark-blue couch in his living room. "I'll just be a minute."

As Dani settled on the couch, he hurried to his bedroom to retrieve a backup phone charger. He really needed to buy a new cell since this battery was shot. He just hadn't taken the time to do so yet.

Just as he grabbed the charger from his dresser, someone knocked at his front door.

His shoulders tensed. Who would be stopping by here unannounced?

He hoped trouble hadn't followed him home.

Levi's hand went to his gun as he stepped back into the living room. He motioned for Dani to stay on the couch and out of sight.

Then he pulled the door open.

Mary Lou stood there, something in her hands.

"It's a cake," she crooned, stepping inside without invitation. "Just for you."

"For me?" Levi repeated, his throat tightening.

"That's right. It's lemon—your favorite. I've been practicing for the church bakeoff that's coming up in a couple of weeks. I thought you might enjoy one of my practice cakes."

"That's awfully nice of you."

Mary Lou started to say something when her gaze flew across the room. She froze.

"I . . . I didn't realize you had company." Her cheeks reddened.

"We just stopped by to grab something." Levi started to introduce them, but he didn't want too many people to know Dani's name.

"I see." Mary Lou pointed behind her. "I guess I should get going."

"Thanks for the cake," Levi called.

"Anytime." She wiggled her fingers in the air. "Take care."

Before she walked away, she handed Levi something. "Oh, and this note was on your porch."

Levi took it from her and nodded. "Thanks."

But as he opened the envelope, his face tensed. Dani glanced over his shoulder and saw the words there. BACK OFF.

It was obviously a threat. But what did that mean? Did it involve Dani? Or was there something else going on here?

CHAPTER SEVENTEEN

DANI REMEMBERED the look of surprise on the woman's face.

Mary Lou obviously hadn't expected to see Dani here, nor had Levi expected her to show up. What exactly was their relationship? Dani didn't think it was romantic... at least not on Levi's end.

Levi turned to Dani and offered an apologetic frown. "Sorry about that."

"It's no problem."

He held up the cake in his hands. "Maybe I'll share this with Emmy and the gang later."

"Twelve layers, huh?"

"It's one of the things this island is known for—their cakes. Everyone is always trying to outdo everyone else by coming up with a better recipe. I always say you don't mess with something that's not broken."

"It makes sense to me." Dani wondered exactly what Levi and Mary Lou's history was.

She also wondered about the woman in the photos with Levi.

She'd seen a couple of the pictures. Levi had looked so happy, almost like a different person. His eyes had glowed as the two of them posed together on the beach.

The woman had been a blonde with long, flowing hair and a bright, wholesome smile.

Dani should have known that someone like Levi would have a girlfriend. But where was that woman now? Dani had met several of Levi's other friends and family on the island. Perhaps Dani would meet her later.

"You ready to go?" Levi asked. "You look like you could use some rest."

Now that he mentioned it, Dani could use more shuteye. The trauma her body had gone through left her exhausted. Though this morning's excursion had been nice, it had also drained the little bit of energy Dani had.

As she looked at Levi, she tried to express with her gaze just how grateful she was for everything he'd done.

"Thank you for going above and beyond." Her voice quivered with emotion.

"It's no problem." Levi offered a polite nod, though his eyes seemed to indicate that he truly cared—despite the boundaries he'd put in place. "Let's get going."

Dani stepped outside and toward the Jeep, ready to head to her temporary home.

But she knew the truth. She was a girl without a home. Without a family. And without friends.

The realization did nothing to comfort her, but only reminded her of the hole that existed in her heart.

AS SOON AS Levi stepped into the Community Safety Headquarters building, he spotted Grant and Dash, another officer, at one of the three desks that were set up near the entry.

"Anything new?" Levi strode toward them.

"Answers are coming in slower than a snail crawling through molasses." Grant frowned as he looked up. "How about you?"

"Dani didn't remember anything. We know no more today than we did yesterday."

"That's disappointing." Dash lifted his cowboy hat and brushed his sandy-colored hair back before placing it back on his head. The man was thin but strong. He had a quick smile, suave mannerisms, and intelligent eyes.

He was one of the newer members of their team, but Dash had proven to be trustworthy and reliable. Despite those qualities, Levi still sensed something secretive about the man, like there were parts of his past he didn't want to share.

In good time, maybe Dash would trust the rest of the gang enough to open up.

There were only three people who worked here for the Forestry Division—Levi, Grant, and Dash. The fire station only had one full-time firefighter—Chief Clint Blackwell. The other firefighters were volunteers. They also had a dispatcher who worked in the office full time and a part-time administrative assistant.

Levi stopped in front of the desk, trying to sort through all his thoughts. "It is disappointing, though not totally unexpected. Two strangers. No IDs." He shook his head.

As he said the words, Dani's picture flashed into his mind. Levi imagined her standing on the sand dune this morning. Envisioned her long, dark hair being carried with the breeze. Remembered the grief in her gaze when she inquired if anyone had come forward to identify her.

The woman was fascinating—and that wasn't something he often said.

Stay your distance, he reminded himself.

That's exactly what he planned on doing.

"Good news is that we got ballistics back on that bullet that was pulled out of Dani." Grant straightened. "It came from a Glock but didn't match anything on file."

Levi nodded as he processed that. "What about fingerprints? Have we run Dani's through the system yet? John Doe's?"

"We have, for both the amnesia victim and for our dead guy," Dash said. "Nothing has come up yet, though. I'll let you know if and when we get a hit."

Levi crossed his arms and leaned against his desk. "What about Skeeter? Any updates?"

Dash shook his head. "We have people on the lookout for him. But no one's seen him."

"What about his momma?" Levi continued.

"I saw her this morning—alone," Grant said.

Levi frowned. "That's not good."

"It's not," Grant said. "But we'll keeping looking. We've still got a little time before this becomes an emergency."

Grant was correct, but worry still coursed through Levi.

"Has anyone talked to Acadia yet?" Levi sat at his desk, knowing he had paperwork he needed to work on. He'd get to that later. Right now, he had to concentrate on their active investigations.

"She's with KitKat," Dash said. "The horse has been standing in the same place for two days. Acadia is afraid she has a snake bite."

Levi frowned.

He was going to let Acadia concentrate on KitKat for the time being. Right now, Levi needed to make a call to Dr. Knightly and see if he had any updates for him.

Things had gone from peaceful and relaxing here on this island, where their biggest concern had been their annual oyster festival, to total chaos.

Before he could leave to go to the clinic, the door opened and Dr. Knightly strode inside. His sun-bleached hair was pulled into a neat ponytail near his neck and his nose was red, like he'd forgotten to use sunscreen last time he'd been surfing. Despite his beach-bum look, his gaze clearly stated he was here on business.

"I thought I'd save you the trip down to the office," he started. "I had to come out this way anyway."

"What's going on?" Levi pointed to an empty chair in front of his desk.

Dr. Knightly sat down and held up a folder in his hands. "First of all, it looks like the cause of death for our John Doe was blunt force trauma to the head. My original theory was correct. The man was kicked in the ribcage, which probably took him down. Then he received a fatal blow to the head."

"By a horse?" Dash asked.

"By a horse." Dr. Knightly pulled out some

photos and showed them the bruising. "You can clearly see this is a hoof print."

This wasn't what Levi wanted to hear.

"Do you think we'll be able to match the print to the horse?" Grant moved closer and glanced at the photos.

"I'm going to have to ask someone above my pay grade about that," Levi said. "I've never had to do this before, so I'm not sure."

Levi knew that a hoof print could be just as distinct as a fingerprint. But with bruising, it would be hard to say exactly what the hoof print looked like.

"I'd say he died just after midnight," Knightly continued. "There were drugs in his system. That's about all I can tell you."

"Thanks for your help, Dr. Knightly." Levi appreciated just how thorough the doctor was.

He nodded but made no effort to leave. "It's no problem. How is our amnesia victim?"

Levi remembered his visit with Dani this morning. "She's hanging in. But she hasn't recalled anything yet."

"It can take time. Sometimes, memories can be triggered. Sometimes, memories don't come back at all. It's great that you're letting her stay at the inn, though. I think she'll be a lot happier there than she would have been at the clinic."

"Let's hope so."

As the doctor left, Levi's mind raced through everything he knew about this case.

He still had a lot of work to do.

Starting with trying to figure out the identity of their victim as well as Dani's.

CHAPTER EIGHTEEN

DANI TRIED to take a nap back at the inn, but she mostly tossed and turned. Not even taking some pain medication helped. She had too much on her mind. Her shoulder hurt. And that feeling of being lost haunted her.

Finally, after an hour of restlessness, she headed downstairs. Maybe she could find something to do to keep her thoughts occupied.

As soon as she rounded the corner, she spotted Emmy working in the kitchen.

"Hey," Dani called, pausing by the breakfast bar.

Emmy turned from organizing one of the cabinets and flashed a smile at her. "You're awake."

"I am." Dani glanced at all the contents of the cabinets scattered on the counter. "Can I help you with anything down here?"

Emmy shrugged and wiped her hands on a paper towel. "I'm just trying to get the kitchen cleaned. Most people do spring cleaning. I prefer to do spring cleaning and fall cleaning. I can't stand a disorganized cabinet."

"I probably shouldn't climb on a ladder," Dani nodded toward the sling around her arm, "but I can definitely help clean out the drawers or the bottom cabinets if you want."

"Okay then. I'm never one to turn down help." Emmy tossed her a rag.

Dani went to a drawer and began pulling things out so she could wipe down the bottom. It would be nice to keep her mind occupied for a while. She had a feeling she was the type who liked to stay busy.

"Not to sound like a broken record, but I really appreciate you letting me stay." Dani meant the words. What would she do if it wasn't for the hospitality of the people here in Cape Corral?

"Of course. Until you regain your memory, you can't exactly be released into the wild." Emmy flashed a smile. "Excuse my wording. I think of everything in terms of horses, though."

"I'd like to earn my keep somehow. Maybe I could help with breakfast or with cleaning. Whatever you need." It only seemed fair.

"You don't have to worry about that." Emmy wiped down another shelf in the cabinet.

"I know. But I would like to. It would be nice to earn my keep—at least until I can repay you." Dani might not know a lot about herself, but there were some qualities that seemed ingrained in her, qualities like work ethic and the need to be useful.

"I'm not worried about you repaying me."

"Then let me give you a hand."

Emmy stared at her another moment before nodding. "Okay then. It would be nice to have some help around here. You've got a deal."

They worked quietly beside each other for a few minutes. As they did, Dani's thoughts raced ahead. What was life like here on this island? The place seemed so secluded and cut off from the rest of the world. Was that a good thing or a bad thing?

"So, Officer Sutherland is your brother?" Dani pulled out some pots and pans from the bottom shelf.

Emmy snorted. "It sounds so serious when you say his name that way. I prefer just Levi."

The words had been spoken like only a sister could speak them. "So, is it just the two of you?"

"Just the two of us."

"It sounds like you must really love living here if you've stayed," Dani said.

"I do. There's nowhere else I'd rather be. These horses are my life. Most of my friends from high school were out of here as soon as they got their diplomas. Not me. I couldn't be dragged away."

"That sounds nice to love a place so much." Dani told the truth.

She wanted to imagine what it would be like to find a place where she fit. Even though it had only been a day since Dani had lost her memory, nothing in her life felt settled. It wouldn't until she knew who she was and what had happened to her.

"Yeah, it is." Emmy continued to pull glasses from a top shelf. "My dad and I never thought that Levi would end up back here. But he did. Mostly because of Adrienne."

Dani's interest perked at the new piece of information. "Who is Adrienne?"

Emmy's face reddened. "I probably shouldn't have brought her up. But Adrienne was Levi's wife. She died in a horseback riding accident."

Dani sucked in a breath. She'd had no idea.

Dani couldn't imagine how difficult it would be to lose a spouse. It sounded . . . horrible.

"I'm sorry to hear that," she murmured.

"We all were. Adrienne was a great woman. There was nothing not to like about her, and we all felt her loss for the longest time. Afterward, Levi just threw himself into his work."

"I'm sure that's a natural thing to do when you're trying to forget." The irony of Dani's words wasn't lost on her. Some people would do anything to forget; Dani would do anything to remember.

Emmy nodded. "I imagine you're right. Staying busy can be good therapy."

Just then, somebody stepped through the back door.

Colby.

"Look what I found outside." He lifted something in his hands.

Dani's eyes widened when she saw the snake.

Emmy gasped and climbed down from the counter, backing into a corner. "Colby Morris, you get that critter out of here. Right now."

Colby grinned, the action almost looking rakish. "But I thought you liked snakes."

Emmy backed farther into a corner. "You know good and well that I hate snakes. Now you get that critter out of here, Colby Devin Morris."

The man didn't seem deterred. In fact, his grin grew even wider.

"Do I have to?" He crept closer.

The next instant, Emmy squealed and ran into the other room. Colby chased after her.

Dani fought a smile at their antics and tried to push away the tinge of jealousy she felt.

It must be nice to belong.

To have people who would miss you if you were gone.

Just what kind of person had she been that no one had even reported her absence? The question echoed in her.

Her heart panged.

Maybe she didn't want to know.

LEVI SPENT the rest of the afternoon canvassing the area for anybody who might be able to identify either Dani or John Doe. He'd also searched for Skeeter.

So far, he'd found nothing and no one.

He didn't like the sound of that. Certainly, someone here on the island had seen something.

He paused near the North Banks and surveyed the area in front of him.

This area was where the Fergusons had started to buy up land to build their mega mansions. These houses didn't fit the rest of the landscape. Instead, they were extravagant three-story structures with swimming pools and elevators.

Though Levi had jurisdiction on the entire island, he'd never felt welcome in this part of the community. He was sure the Fergusons intended it that way.

However, many vacationers stayed in the North Banks. Levi knew he needed to talk to some people in this area if he wanted to find answers, and he certainly wasn't going to be deterred by the lack of friendliness from the Fergusons.

He canvased the area, showing residents the

picture of their John Doe. Most people shook their heads no and indicated that they hadn't seen anything.

As he saw Abigail Ferguson walking toward her expensive Jeep, he flagged her down. "Abigail!"

The woman stopped and looked around, as if uncomfortable in his presence. Abigail was the daughter of the patriarch of the Ferguson family. She was pretty with long, ash-blonde hair and aristocratic features. Something about her seemed different than the rest of her clan. Her edges weren't as hard, her arrogance not as prominent, and her gaze not as standoffish.

She raised her chin as she turned to address him. "Levi. What's going on?"

Levi showed her the pictures. "Have you seen either of these two around here?"

She studied the photos for a moment before shaking her head. "I can't say I have. Is everything okay?"

Levi nodded and shifted as he stood there on the sandy road. "I'm just doing some investigative work."

She paused and studied his face a moment. "I heard about the dead body Mom found last night."

"I figured the news was all over the island by now."

She nodded. "I ran into Grant this morning, and he told me."

Levi's eyes narrowed. Abigail and Grant had been talking? That was interesting. Why in the world would Grant want to talk to Abigail Ferguson?

He'd think about the question later.

"If you hear about anything strange that's been happening on the island, please let me know," Levi finally said.

"I will."

Just as Levi started to walk away, Abigail called to him, "Wait."

He turned back to her.

She glanced around again before stepping closer. "I was out two mornings ago riding my four-wheeler. I like to go back into Wash Woods. It's . . . it's peaceful back there. Anyway, I saw some people camping back there."

Levi's jaw tightened. "Camping is illegal here on the island."

"I know. I'm not saying I condoned it." She offered a tense shrug. "I'm just saying I saw a tent set up, and I saw some people inside. I didn't see any faces. But you might want to check it out. They might know something."

Levi definitely wanted to check that out. "Do you remember exactly what area the dune was located in?"

"It wasn't far from the Jezebel Tree."

The blood drained from Levi's face. He wasn't superstitious, but many people on the island were.

Stories about that tree went back for decades. Longer than decades. The stories went back generations.

Rumors had made their rounds about a beautiful woman who'd seduced many of the captains on the island. She'd eventually been found hanging from the tree, and to this day no one knew what had happened to her. Some say a scorned lover did it. Others said a jealous wife. Some said she did it to herself.

Either way, the tree had become legendary.

Ever since then, people had said that the tree was haunted.

Levi didn't believe in any of that.

But it did make for some intriguing island folklore.

"Thanks, Abigail," Levi finally said. "I'll go check that out."

"Good luck, Levi."

He nodded. "Thanks. I might need it."

He'd need more than luck. He needed the grace of God.

CHAPTER NINETEEN

LEVI DIRECTED NELLY toward the Jezebel Tree. Riding horseback had its advantages. His presence was more easily concealed without the hum of a motor giving him away. There was no need to give criminals time to prepare or hide.

Also, Nelly easily navigated between the shrubs. This part of the island—known by locals as Wash Woods—morphed from rugged natural shoreline into the maritime forest. Hills rose where the dunes had once stood. Vegetation had taken over, making the land almost seem like miniature mountains with cliffs and hollows.

The maritime forest had an entirely different ecosystem than other parts of the island, which Levi found fascinating. But the area was also dangerous in its own right. Wild boars, water moccasins, foxes, and even a bear or two were seen inhabiting the area on occasion.

Those wild animals were just one of the many reasons why camping wasn't allowed in these woods. But every year, a few people tried to do it anyway. They tried to buck the system and find a free place to sleep for the night.

Those very same people—those who thought they were above the rules—were usually the ones who ended up leaving litter behind or trying to feed the wild horses. Once, Levi had even caught some college age kids trying to ride one of the wild mares. Thankfully, they hadn't been successful. Instead, they'd ended up with hefty fines, and Levi had to use every ounce of self-control not to lash out at them for their stupidity.

Levi bobbed along, surveying the landscape as he did.

So far, he hadn't seen anything.

But what if these people who'd been staying back here knew Dani? Or the dead man?

For that reason, Levi would keep searching. He'd called Grant as backup, knowing it would take Levi entirely too long to canvas the area by himself.

As he continued to ride, his heart tightened. Adrienne had loved this part of the island. Whenever she came to Wash Woods, she felt like she'd escaped to a deserted, private isle. That's what she'd always said.

Though she'd loved people, she'd also treasured her time alone. Sometimes Levi even suspected she loved horses more than people. He couldn't say he didn't understand the sentiment.

The ache in his heart deepened. It was still so hard to believe that Adrienne was gone. Still so unfair. Levi would do anything to have her back. To share a laugh together. To dream about their future. To have a listening ear, a confidante that only a spouse could be.

They were high school sweethearts who'd married right after college. They'd wanted to start a family together—five kids. Adrienne had wanted to stay home with them. In the meantime, she'd worked at the post office.

Although Levi's grief had possibly lessened and he'd started to feel a new sense of normal, Adrienne's loss would always be with him. He wasn't sure anything would ever change that fact. He wasn't sure he ever wanted it to, for that matter.

He readjusted the cowboy hat as the sun now hung directly overhead, heating the landscape around him like a warming blanket. He'd stay out here another hour or so before taking Nelly back to cool off and rest.

He paused as he reached the Jezebel Tree. The live oak stood alone, with no other trees around it.

Its branches were twisted and gnarled, and it was one of the largest live oaks Levi had ever seen.

If one looked closely enough in the bark, they could make out the name "Jezebel" carved into the wood there. Supposedly, the tree had been there since the 1800s.

Levi let out a sigh.

He'd seen nothing out here so far. Had Abigail been making up things just to waste his time? He didn't want to think so, but it was a possibility.

He could see some of the Fergusons doing that, but he couldn't see Abigail taking their feud that far. Unlike some of her family, Abigail had actually helped a tourist one time who'd fallen off a third-story deck. She'd waited with the man, comforting him, until help had arrived.

The woman seemed to have a slightly bigger heart than the rest of her clan.

But Levi didn't know her well enough to say that with 100 percent certainty. It was best to remain cautious.

At the thought of that, his job offer came to mind again. Could he really see himself leaving this behind? The island had so much character, so much history. What would it be like to get away from this?

To get away from the memories of Adrienne.

That was what it really boiled down to, wasn't it?

The memories.

In fact, the two of them had shared their first kiss right here by this tree when they were in high school. Neither of them had looked at anyone else after that—they'd lived out "until death do us part."

Just then, Grant appeared at the top of the dune on his steed, Brightly. He trotted down to meet Levi.

"Discover any skullduggery?" Grant asked.

Levi shook his head, wishing he had different news. "No, nothing yet."

Grant nodded in the distance. "Have you checked the other side of the dune? By Blackwater Marsh?"

"Not yet." Levi hadn't made it that far yet. "Why don't we ride together?"

They started across the sand side by side. Small ponds that had started out as puddles from rain showers or storm surges graced any low-lying areas. There was nowhere else for the water to go on the island sometimes, except to settle in the crevices between the sand dunes.

That made getting around the place interesting at times, especially as some of the water masses grew larger and deeper. Many tourists tried to drive through those very puddles only to get stuck and flood their engines.

But the puddles also offered the horses a place

to drink. The water wasn't always the freshest, but the horses seemed to prefer it. In all the years Levi had been here, the small ponds hadn't hurt the horses yet.

"So who gave you this tip about the campers out here?" Grant's hand casually gripped the reins in front of him as he steered Brightly around a tree.

Funny that Grant had brought that up . . . "Abigail Ferguson."

Grant's eyebrows shot up before his face went placid—purposefully placid, it seemed. "Did she?"

"She said you told her about our dead body." Levi kept his words casual, though curiosity burned inside him.

Grant's cheeks reddened. "I ran into her this morning while I was running on the beach. She was taking a jog, and our paths happened to cross."

"Is that right?" Levi had a feeling there was more to that story.

Even if their paths had crossed, that didn't seem like a good reason to strike up conversation. Not considering the feud between her family and the locals. Besides, why had Grant been jogging up on the north end of the island? Had he been hoping to run into the woman?

"She wants to start rehabilitating the sea turtles that come up in the area," Grant continued, giving his collar a small tug. "We met together several weeks ago to talk about it."

"Funny that this is the first time you're mentioning it." There was definitely more to this story. Otherwise, why wouldn't Grant have said something?

"It's off the books, nothing official. I was just giving her my opinion as a wildlife officer."

"That was generous of you." Levi tried to keep the humor out of his voice.

Grant remained quiet.

Before Levi could ask him any more questions, something caught his eye up ahead.

A tent.

Grant and Levi glanced at each other.

It looked like they had found their intruders.

Now Levi needed to find out what they knew.

"SO HOW LONG HAVE YOU and Colby been dating?" Dani asked Emmy as they rearranged the silverware drawer.

"Colby and me?" Emmy's eyes widened. "Oh, we aren't dating. We're just friends."

Surprise washed through Dani. "Oh, I'm sorry. I just assumed—"

"It's no problem. Sometimes people think we're together—romantically—because we spend so much time attached at the hip. But I practically think of him as a brother."

"Well, he seems nice."

Emmy polished another fork. "He's a great guy. Some girl will be lucky one day."

Dani smiled. The two of them seemed to have a cozy friendship.

"So, can you see yourself sticking around here for a while?" Emmy asked.

Dani blinked, not expecting the question. "I . . . I don't know. I just assume I'll return to my old life eventually. Soon, I hope. Not that I haven't enjoyed it here. Other than being shot, of course."

"Of course." Emmy frowned. "I'm sorry you can't remember any details of your life."

"Me too."

"I suppose some people would like the idea of getting a totally fresh start."

Dani let out a chuckle. "It's unnerving, nothing close to glamorous or romantic like the movies make it seem."

"Of course. I shouldn't have implied that."

Dani dropped a spoon she held. As it clattered to the floor, she reached down to pick it up. When she did, she caught a glimpse of her ankles. There were scratches there. Scratches and bug bites.

"Everything okay?" Emmy appeared beside her, dismounting the ladder in three seconds flat.

Dani rose. "I think so. It's just . . . I hadn't noticed my ankles yet. There are dozens of mosquito bites there."

"Sounds like you spent time outside."

"Could they have happened when I washed up on the beach?"

Emmy shrugged. "Maybe. But mosquitoes usually aren't right there by the ocean. They're generally on the sound side more."

"I guess the scratches could have come from shells in the breakwater."

Emmy leaned closer, her eyes narrowing with thought. "Maybe. To me, it looks like you were taking a hike or something."

Taking a hike? What sense would that make?

The questions continued to swirl in Dani's mind.

CHAPTER TWENTY

THE TENT WAS empty other than some sleeping bags, but its inhabitants had obviously been here recently. The embers in the firepit were still warm, and they'd found a bag of fresh trash inside. The trash was a sure sign these campers were amateurs. You never left food scraps inside a tent—if you didn't want to attract wildlife.

Levi knew that, most likely, these guys had headed toward the sound access. The Currituck was the closest body of water, and most people would want to cool off on a warm day like this.

He and Grant quietly trotted in that direction. As they got closer, the sound of voices rose in the air.

Levi slowed his horse's steps and motioned for Grant to remain quiet.

As soon as they crossed beyond the trees, they

spotted two men. The men lounged on rafts in the water with beer bottles in hand. Occasionally, they splashed each other or made a lewd joke. If Levi had to guess, they were college age—frat boys, probably.

Levi felt certain that these were the men he was looking for.

Remaining on horseback, Levi nudged Nelly toward the shore.

"Excuse me." Levi lifted the edge of his shirt so they could see the badge at his waistband. "I'm Officer Sullivan with the Forestry Division. I need to ask you a few questions."

As one of the guys turned toward Levi, he tumbled from the raft and splashed into the water. Levi watched in amusement as the man surfaced a moment later. He coughed and ran a hand over his wet face.

Finally, the man stood, water dripping from his skin as he stepped closer. "What can I do for you, officer?"

His friend also stood, however, much more gracefully. He grabbed his raft and stepped toward the sandy shore.

"Do either of you know anything about the tent that's set up about fifty feet from here?" Levi asked.

Without either of them saying a word, Levi knew the campsite was theirs. Both of their bodies had tensed as he asked the question.

"A tent?" Dripping Wet Man repeated with a shrug. "No, I don't know anything about any tent. Do you, Gilbert?"

"Nah, man. We're just out here enjoying the water for a while. That's not a crime, is it?"

"It's not," Levi said. "Where are you two staying while you're in town? I don't remember seeing either of you before."

Dripping Wet Man shrugged again. "We have a small rental just in town."

"What street?" Grant pushed.

The man let out a nervous chuckle. "It's hard to say, especially since there aren't really streets signs around here."

"Yet there *are* street names for when visitors come to the island." Levi wasn't letting them off the hook that easily. "They show up on your GPS so you can find your correct location."

"I don't know." Gilbert's face reddened, like his friend was irritating him. "Maybe Main Street."

"There's no Main Street here." Levi crossed his arms. "Now, why don't you two tell the truth? Is that your tent back there?"

Neither of the men said anything for a moment before finally Dripping Wet Man nodded. "It is. We didn't mean any harm by staying out here."

"Barry!" Gilbert said, reprimand in his voice.

Barry shrugged.

"It's a good thing that neither of you got yourself killed," Levi told them. "Last time I caught some campers out here, a wild boar found them before I did."

Barry and Gilbert both went a little paler.

"We just wanted a little getaway," Barry rushed. "We weren't going to take anything or leave anything, as the saying goes."

People who broke one rule usually weren't hesitant about breaking others—as long as the regulations seemed inconsequential to them. That had been Levi's experience.

"We have a few questions you're going to need to answer," Levi continued.

The two men looked at each other.

Levi braced himself, sensing what would happen next.

Right on cue, Barry and Gilbert took off, sprinting down the shoreline.

CHAPTER TWENTY-ONE

LEVI ONLY HAD to nod at Grant to indicate what their plan was. The next second, Grant took off through the woods as Levi trailed behind the men on horseback.

If these men really thought they were going to be able to run faster than Levi's and Grant's horses, they needed a better education.

Before Barry and Gilbert made it twenty feet, Grant appeared in front of them. The two men stopped in their tracks. They started to turn, but, as they did, they nearly collided with Levi and realized they were trapped.

Barry held his hands in the air. "Okay, okay. I can see that wasn't a good idea."

"My patience is running out," Levi started.

"I wouldn't lollygag if I were you," Grant said.

"You don't want to see him when his patience runs out."

"You two need to start talking. Now what's going on? What are you doing out here?"

"We don't want to get in trouble," Barry started. "My friend and I just wanted to take a camping trip."

"That's not what we're out here to ask you about," Levi started.

The two men stared at him cautiously.

"Then what is it?" Gilbert asked.

"I need to know if you saw this man." Levi found John Doe's picture on his phone and held it out to the men.

They only had to study it a moment before Gilbert nodded. "Yes, we saw him."

Levi's interest perked. Maybe they'd finally make some progress. "Where did you see him?"

"He and some other people climbed off a boat at one of these docks nearby and were walking through the forest," Barry said.

"Some other people?" Grant asked.

"There were three of them," Gilbert said. "Two men and a woman."

Levi's heart jumped into his throat. Though he had no personal connection with Dani, he'd still somehow hoped she was innocent in this.

"Did the woman look like this?" Levi showed the men her picture.

Barry nodded. "That was her."

The lump in Levi's throat grew larger. "I need to know everything about them. And don't tell me you don't have time to talk. If you do, I'll add obstruction of justice to your list of crimes."

"We'll tell you whatever you need," Gilbert said. "Please, don't arrest us. Or fine us. Please. We'll cooperate."

"Yes, you will." Levi would make sure that happened.

DANI SAT at the kitchen table after they organized the cabinets and made a list of groceries for Emmy —at Emmy's request. Emmy wanted to have a coffee and tea bar set up in the corner for guests to utilize whenever they wanted.

Apparently, trips into town to the grocery store were something that required a lot of planning since there was only a small market here on the island. Emmy said that list was everything when it came to making her life easier here in Cape Corral.

Emmy was outside on the back porch painting an old buffet table with white chalk paint while Dani brainstormed some ideas for the coffee bar— sweeteners, creamers, biscotti.

As Dani glanced down at the paper and pen in front of her, she froze.

A memory tried to stir.

She could hardly breathe as she waited for it to emerge.

But nothing came.

Dani squeezed her eyes shut and waited.

What was it? What had teased the edge of her recall?

She tried to force herself to remember, but it didn't work. No flashbacks appeared in her memory.

But something had been there. Had been on the verge of emerging.

Dani stared at the pen and paper in her hands again. Maybe she had been a reporter. Would that explain the physical reaction she was having to seeing this pen in her hands?

She didn't know. And she hated not knowing.

"Everything okay?" Emmy stepped inside, paintbrush in hand, and paused by the table where Dani sat.

Dani forced a smile, not wanting this perfect stranger who'd kindly taken her in to worry about her any more than Emmy already had been. "Just fine. Tired, I suppose."

"Do you need to go rest?"

"No, I'm fine. I still think it's better if I keep moving forward."

"I appreciate all your help today." Emmy took a step back but paused. "By the way, we're having a bonfire outside Colby's place tonight. You should come."

A bonfire? The idea sounded nice, normal even. But . . . "I would hate to intrude on your time with your friends."

"I think it would be good for you," Emmy said. "I know that when I'm trying to sort my thoughts out, there are two things that I always do. One is watching the ocean waves as they pound the shore. And the other is watching a fire as it crackles and reaches into the air. You've already tried the ocean. Why not give the other a try?"

Dani liked the way Emmy thought.

After another moment, she finally nodded. "If I'm feeling up to it, maybe I will. Thank you for the invitation."

But another part of Dani hoped that at any minute, somebody would show up and claim her. That she wouldn't have to spend another night here. That she could go home and her life would return to normal.

Was she hoping for too much?

Her shoulders sagged.

At times, that was exactly what it felt like.

CHAPTER TWENTY-TWO

LEVI CALLED Dash to come with the Jeep, and they took Gilbert Lancaster and Barry Stephens to his office.

Both were nineteen years old and from the Hampton Roads area of Virginia. According to them, they'd come to Cape Corral three days ago to camp, and their ride was supposed to be picking them up via boat tomorrow.

Both men had said that, around six or seven p.m. two days ago, they'd seen two men and a woman being dropped off on a sound-side dock. The group had talked as if they were friends as they'd trekked through the woods.

Neither Gilbert nor Barry had been able to make out any of the conversation, but both said the group didn't seem to be at odds with each other as they disappeared into the woods.

Levi had given both men a warning before Grant took them to pick up their belongings in Wash Woods. Meanwhile, their ride had been called so they could vacate the island sooner than expected.

The two of them just seemed happy to be walking away without any charges.

But as Levi sat at his desk and let everything he'd learned sink in he only had more questions. He tapped his pen against his desk as he stared at an old beach painting that his dad had left here when he'd retired.

He frowned.

Just as Levi had suspected, Dani *was* in some way mixed up in whatever had happened here on the island. Two men had been with her—including their dead man.

But why? Why were they here?

The only reason someone would sneak onto the island via boat would be if they were up to trouble. But something had clearly happened between the time Dani and the men had arrived and when they'd left.

The only way that Dani's body could have washed up from the ocean was if this group had gotten back in the boat and cut through one of the inlets to the Atlantic. Levi would guess that their John Doe had never made it back to the boat but that he'd died while here on the island.

He had a lot of questions and not a lot of answers. But he really hoped that Dani wasn't on the wrong side of the law.

He closed the folder where he'd been putting together his report and then rubbed a hand over his eyes.

It had been a long day, and the end was still not in sight.

AGAINST HER BETTER INSTINCTS, Dani decided to go to the campfire that evening. Mostly, she didn't want to stay at the inn by herself. Which was stupid. This island seemed perfectly safe.

But every time she thought about that, she remembered the gunshot wound in her shoulder and the bruise on her cheek. She couldn't be too careful at times like this.

Emmy had packed up the ingredients for s'mores in a little picnic basket before the two of them started down the road together.

It was already dark outside. Really dark. Without any streetlights, nothing illuminated their way except for the little flashlights they carried.

"So you'll get to meet the whole gang tonight," Emmy said, swinging the basket in her hand.

Another moment of envy struck Dani when she saw Emmy's carefree attitude. She hoped that one day she might get to that point. But not right now. Not with so many uncertainties.

"Who exactly is the whole gang?" Dani asked.

"My brother will be there along with his best friend, Grant. Dash will probably be there as well. He's one of the newest members of the Forestry Law Enforcement team here on the island. Colby, of course, will be there since it's at his place. And there will be a few other guys and gals who work with the horses or in Fire and Rescue."

"It's nice that you can get together like this. Do you do things like this often?"

"We try to have a bonfire together once a week. It's a way to blow off steam. It's not like there are movie theaters around here or baseball games or anything else that the average person in the average town might entertain themselves with."

"But you have horses and the ocean, so it's not all bad."

A smile lit Emmy's face. "Exactly. What more could you want? That's what I always say."

They walked a few more moments in silence. But the quiet didn't last long. In the background, the sound of someone playing an acoustic guitar, as well as chatter among friends, floated through the air.

A few minutes later, Dani and Emmy turned and headed behind one of the houses. A group had gathered around the fire in a corner of the property near the woods. Makeshift benches had been set up with cinder blocks and wooden boards around the firepit.

Everybody in the circle looked so happy as they talked or sang.

Dani paused as envy once again rushed through her.

What she wouldn't do to have that type of camaraderie with someone right now. Had she ever had it? Or had she been a loner? What if she'd been unlikable and hadn't had friends? Or if she'd been a workaholic? She had so many questions, but those inquiries weren't louder than her desire to belong.

Despite that longing, Dani knew she had a lot to be grateful for. Thank God she had a place to stay and food to eat until she figured things out.

A few people called hello, and Emmy introduced her to everyone in the group.

As Dani's gaze searched the circle, she realized Levi wasn't here.

Her heart sank, almost in disappointment.

Disappointment? What sense did that make? Dani shouldn't be disappointed if the man wasn't there. As she often had to remind herself, he was simply the man who'd rescued her and nothing more. She'd be foolish to think their bond went any deeper.

She settled on a bench to watch and observe.

This gathering was nice, she decided. For a moment it almost felt like she'd been swept back in time to a different era—an era where simple things were paramount. Where friends were a priority. Where life had a slower pace.

She wasn't sure where the thoughts came from—except for deep down in her soul.

If only Dani could remember who she was, then maybe she could find herself enjoying this. But until she had answers, she would remain on edge.

CHAPTER TWENTY-THREE

LEVI ALMOST HADN'T COME to the bonfire at Colby's place. But Emmy had texted him several times asking him where he was.

He struggled with finding his work/personal life balance, especially since Adrienne died. This bonfire would be an easy way to break away from his desk and all the paperwork that waited for him there. Maybe he could clear his head for a few minutes.

As soon as he rounded the corner of Colby's house, he paused and soaked in the sight of his friends gathered around laughing and talking. Sticks extended over the fire, with puffy marshmallows on the ends. Carefree music played over a speaker somewhere.

His gaze stopped on Dani.

She was here.

For a moment, he forgot about the woman's possible role in something nefarious going on here on the island. Instead, he was captivated by the glow of the fire on her skin. Her long, wavy hair fell over her shoulders. After a moment, she smiled, almost as if she'd been part of this group for a long time.

But the smile quickly disappeared as she stared into the flames again.

No doubt she had a lot on her mind.

Had she remembered anything? Levi would need to check in with her again about that later. For now, he would let her enjoy herself.

It still bothered him that nobody had come forward looking for her. Levi had checked all the missing person reports, and there had been nothing about her or anyone who fit her description.

He knew there could be a logical explanation, but most people noticed their loved ones were gone by now. They noticed that there hadn't been any phone calls or communication. Mail piled up. Absences from work were noticed.

Just what was Dani's story?

Looking at her now, Levi had a hard time believing that she was up to anything less than savory. Her eyes had an innocent look that couldn't be faked. Then why was she with those men?

"Hey, Levi!"

Levi snapped from his thoughts and glanced at Grant as his friend called him over.

He set his reservations aside. For now.

Instead, he started to the circle. As he did, his friends parted so he could sit next to Dani.

He lowered himself on the bench and offered a slight smile. "Evening."

"Evening," Dani echoed, still turning her marshmallow over the fire.

"It's going to get burnt." He pointed to the puffy blob of sugar as flames licked the edges.

"That's the way I like it." She shrugged. "And don't ask me how I know that. I just do."

Trauma could wreak havoc on a person's memories. He knew that. Dani would definitely need to follow up with the doctor soon, just to make sure her recovery was still on track.

But for now, Levi was going to let that go. Maybe the best thing for Dani was just to have an evening to kick back and relax.

Maybe that would be best for them all.

CHAPTER TWENTY-FOUR

BOBBY PAUSED in the shadow of an old, gnarled tree and glanced down the sandy street in the distance.

He'd been searching the island ever since he arrived last night. So far, he hadn't seen any signs of Dani—or her body.

He hadn't been able to ask any locals directly about her. He'd thought about doing so. Thought about wandering into the one and only restaurant in town and claiming to be a friend.

But if Dani had somehow survived what had happened, no doubt she would have told the police about their plan. Authorities would be out here searching for Bobby and his crew now. That's why he'd decided to operate under the cover of darkness.

Sweat sprinkled across Bobby's forehead as he

thought about it. How had he turned into a criminal? This hadn't been how he intended his life to go. But there was no way out now. Instead, he kept digging his hole deeper and deeper.

He drew in a deep breath and continued walking the streets. No one could hear him coming because the sand acted as his accomplice.

He wasn't sure what he thought he might see at this hour. If Dani was alive and she was here, he thought most likely she'd be at the clinic being kept alive by machines. Maybe paramedics had life flighted her to Norfolk or Raleigh.

But Bobby had called both of those hospitals, and they hadn't been able to give him any information. He'd even come up with a cover story.

It hadn't worked.

Wherever he turned, he hit a dead end.

The Captain would be calling tomorrow and would demand an update on the situation. Too much time was wasting away—and time was something they didn't have right now. His boss wanted this job done and over with so they could move on.

Bobby's heart clenched as he remembered how the events had unfolded.

Poor Dani . . . she'd been clueless about what she was getting into. At least, when the truth had been revealed, she'd had the good sense to stand her ground.

Unlike Bobby.

Bobby had tried to turn his life around. He'd spent some time in prison, but once he'd gotten out this last time, he'd vowed to be a different person. He'd met Winona. Carson was born a year later.

Then, in a moment of weakness, he'd taken a hit of heroin. Winona had caught him and kicked him out.

That's when everything started to go downhill.

The Captain saw that as a weakness. He'd exploited it.

Now Bobby was caught in this situation.

He remained on the edges of the road as he walked. He didn't want to be stopped by anyone. Didn't want anybody asking questions or drawing attention to him.

But with every step, the sweat on his brow increased until it dripped down his face.

He paused.

The sound of people talking and laughing drifted from the distance.

As he approached a nearby house, the sound became louder.

Bobby remained behind a tall bush and peered at the back of the property, curious about what was going on and how the locals lived here in Cape Corral.

He spotted a group of people gathered around a bonfire. There had to be at least twelve people there—talking to each other, laughing, roasting marshmallows.

The sight caused envy to well up inside.

It must be nice to be able to kick back and relax like that.

Bobby hadn't experienced that since he'd started working for the Captain. He'd probably never have his life back again, but he had no one to blame for it except himself.

He examined the faces there but didn't see anybody he recognized. Then again, it was dark, and Bobby was far away.

What if Dani was part of them?

Bobby shook his head. What were the odds that she would have made friends this quickly? No, if she wasn't dead, then she was in a hospital, probably in a coma. If not in a coma, then she would have reported what happened. The police would be looking for him.

So far, things were quiet.

He glanced at the circle one more time before continuing down the road. He needed something more definite to tell his boss. He needed a dead body.

But how was he going to get that?

He didn't know. He only knew he needed to tell the Captain that Dani was dead.

CHAPTER TWENTY-FIVE

DANI FELT the heat burning her skin as Levi's arm brushed up against hers.

Why had people assumed that he'd want to sit beside her? It didn't make sense. But Dani wasn't opposed to being near him. In fact, she found comfort in his presence.

Dani just had to remember that he was only assisting her in a professional manner. She couldn't cling to any type of hero complex. Just because the man had saved her life did not mean anything—except that she should be grateful.

As the flames from the bonfire began to fade, the discussion moved from the whole group to smaller, more intimate talks.

Dani glanced around the circle and saw Emmy and Colby giggling about something. Grant and Dash were in a deep conversation about how to air down tires. The other guys had also started talking amongst themselves.

Everyone seemed to appear to have broken into more cozy conversations except for... Levi and Dani.

Finally, Levi cleared his throat and turned to her. "How are you doing, Dani?"

She wasn't quite sure how to answer that. "I've been better. But physically I'm feeling stronger."

"That's good. I'm glad there haven't been any complications with your injury."

She touched her shoulder and remembered the bullet wound there. "Me too."

"Have you recalled anything today? Recovered any memories?"

Dani was glad he'd asked. "Earlier today, I was staring at a pen and piece of paper. I felt like something was just on the edge of my recall. But the memory never did fully emerge. I'm not sure what it could have been."

"Hopefully, as time passes, you'll remember more."

"Let's hope." Dani glanced at Levi, noticing how handsome he looked in the flickering orange light of the bonfire. "How about you? Have you had any luck figuring out what happened to me?"

He drew in a deep breath, like he needed to sort through what he might say.

Finally, he started, "We're following several

leads. I wasn't going to ask you these questions here."

"It's okay if you need to. I understand. I also understand if you'd rather unwind now and ask me later."

He glanced around, seeming to observe how everybody was still caught up in their own conversations. With a resolute nod, he said, "Grant and I came across two men camping in the woods on the west side of the island. They said they saw you with two men two nights ago. Said you all were brought over by boat."

"I was with two men?" Dani's voice rose louder than she had intended it to. She quickly looked at the people in the bonfire circle. No one seemed to notice.

"That's what they said. It was evening when you arrived, and you all walked through the woods as if on a mission."

Dani's head began to pound, and she squeezed the skin between her eyes as she tried to make sense of that update. "Why would I have come to the island so late in the day?"

"That's what we're trying to figure out."

Then a new thought hit her. "Was one of the men . . . ?" She didn't even have to finish the statement.

Levi nodded, his lips pulled down in a grim

frown. "One of the men has been identified as our John Doe."

Her shoulders slumped toward the ground as she shook her head. "I can't believe this."

This was just horrible.

The more time passed, the more Dani wondered if she was involved with something sinister.

She could hardly stand the thought of that. How could she live with herself if that was true?

She didn't know.

LEVI RESISTED the urge to rest his hand on Dani's back and pull her into a side hug.

The woman looked so alone and entirely too weak to be carrying this burden by herself.

But Levi knew there were professional lines he shouldn't cross.

Even if Dani was one of the most beautiful women he'd laid his eyes on since Adrienne.

He sucked in a breath at the thought.

What?

Where had that thought come from? It made no sense he'd even entertain such a thought.

Levi definitely wasn't looking for a relationship, nor was he looking for a quick fling. He was content to be single. If he couldn't have Adrienne, then he'd be alone.

Yet he hadn't felt a rush of attraction to anybody since Adrienne died.

Until now.

He glanced at Dani again as her head bent toward the ground. He could only imagine the tremendous amount of pressure on her. Her eyes squeezed together, and she reached for her shoulder, her fingers brushing the sling.

Finally, after a moment, Levi rested his hand on her back. "It's going to be okay, Dani."

She shook her head, her dark hair falling over the even lines of her face. "Nothing feels okay. What if I've done something terrible?"

"You don't seem like the type who would have done something terrible." Levi probably shouldn't have said that. If Dani *had* disobeyed the law, then he'd have no choice but to arrest her.

But Levi told the truth when he said those words. His gut instinct about the woman indicated Dani wasn't a criminal but instead someone who had been caught in the middle of something dangerous.

Her head swung up until her eyes met his. "You really think that?"

"I do," Levi said quietly. "I usually have a pretty good instinct about these things."

A brief smile fluttered across her lips before

quickly disappearing. "Did those men say that I looked like I was being held captive? Like I was in distress?"

Levi hesitated before shaking his head. "No, they couldn't hear what anybody was saying, but they said the conversation looked pleasant."

Dani let out another groan and rubbed her forehead. "I'll never forgive myself if I did something to put that other man in danger."

"The fact that you were shot makes me think they were trying to do away with you. Maybe you were caught up in some type of trap yourself."

She rubbed her temple again. "Not being able to remember . . . it's horrible."

Funny that she said that because all Levi had been trying to do was to forget.

Yet, on the other hand, he didn't want to erase his time with Adrienne from his memory. He didn't regret even a moment of it. The only thing Levi lamented was not being able to save his wife when she had needed him the most. That was something that he'd never forgive himself for.

"You know, I'm feeling pretty exhausted." Dani let out a deep breath. "I think I need to turn in for the night."

Levi saw the fatigue on her features. Saw the tight lines across her forehead. The way her lips pressed together. How her gaze sagged.

He stood and took Dani's hand to help her to

her feet. Just as quickly, he let go, not wanting to give anybody the wrong idea. "I'll walk you back to the inn."

Her gaze fluttered up to meet his. "Thank you. I really appreciate that. More than you can ever know."

CHAPTER TWENTY-SIX

LEVI INSISTED on walking Dani back to the inn, and she wasn't complaining.

She always felt better when Levi was with her.

As they strolled down the road, she shoved her right hand into the pocket of the sweatshirt Emmy had let her borrow. Thankfully, the two of them were the same size. Emmy had given Dani a few pairs of jeans, some T-shirts, and a couple sweatshirts that she could wear while she was here.

Before Dani and Levi could get involved in any deep conversation, Levi's phone rang. He excused himself as he answered. He muttered several things into his cell before ending the call and slipping his phone back into his pocket.

Dani sensed something was different after that phone call.

"Is everything okay?" she asked.

"That was the lab. There was a dark hair found on our John Doe."

Dani's lungs froze as she anticipated what he might say next. "And?"

He glanced at her. "It matches the sample of hair we took of yours at the hospital."

She rubbed her throat, not liking the sound of that. "That's not what I wanted to hear."

"I know."

"This doesn't mean that you're going to arrest me or something, does it?"

Levi glanced around as they walked. "No arrests need to be made. We don't believe that a person killed him, so this isn't an active murder investigation."

"But you said his body was found buried beneath the sand dune."

"Someone will face charges for that. Obstruction of justice. But not murder. Not yet at least."

She shivered and shoved her free hand deeper into her sweatshirt pocket. "This confirms that I was definitely connected with that man. I don't like the sound of that."

"I know. But at least a clearer picture is coming together."

"Is it?"

Levi slowed his steps. "Well, we now know you were with two men two nights ago. You arrived on the island by boat. You walked with them through Wash Woods."

"Okay . . ." She failed to see how this was good news.

"John Doe was close enough to one of our wild horses to be kicked. The blow was fatal. Someone —or several someones—then decided to bury his body instead of calling for help."

Bile churned in Dani's gut. The picture forming wasn't something she welcomed.

"Okay." She needed to hear the rest, whether she wanted to or not.

"Sometime after that happened, I imagine the two of you who were left went back to the boat that was docked at the Currituck Sound. You must have taken it out into the ocean. That's where someone shot you and you fell into the water. I found you when you washed ashore the next morning."

"That sounds like nothing but trouble."

"It definitely sounds like you got caught up in something."

Dani flung her gaze toward him, desperate to read the emotion in his face. "But does that mean that I'm guilty?"

Levi slowed his steps even more as he turned toward her. "That's what we're trying to figure out."

Dani noticed that Levi didn't deny that she might be guilty of something.

And she didn't like the sound of that.

She needed answers now more than ever.

AS LEVI WENT downstairs after walking Dani up to her room, he spotted Emmy enter the inn.

"Back so soon?" He paused in front of her, the smoky scent of her hair wafting through the air.

"Our fire went out, so I figured that was a sign it was time to come home."

He glanced behind her. "No Colby?"

"He walked me home, but he wanted to get back so he could talk about that fishing trip with the guys."

"I see." Levi nodded up the stairs. "Everything going okay here with your new guest?"

He needed to know if Dani had opened up to his sister. As much as he just wanted to be a brother and a friend, he still had a job to do. If a potential killer was on this island, Levi needed to find him.

"Oh, she's great." Emmy's eyes lit up, clearly showing she meant the words. "Dani helped me reorganize the kitchen today, and she did an amazing job. Maybe she was a professional organizer before all this happened."

"Maybe." Levi's smile only lasted a second. "She didn't show any signs that she remembered anything, did she?"

"She didn't seem to. Why?" Emmy lowered her voice. "You don't believe her?"

"I'm just trying to cover every angle." Levi kept his voice even, not wanting to share too much or to paint Dani in a bad light.

Emmy tilted her head as she observed him. "That's my brother. Always covering every angle."

"Is that a veiled insult?" He raised an eyebrow.

"Never said it was an insult. And I never said it was veiled." She flashed a smile.

Any other time, he might jab her back. She was his little sister, and Levi had moved from picking on her to watching out for her to simply being friends. Sometimes, he slid back into his old ways just for fun.

He wished he could have a lighthearted moment now. But he couldn't.

Not with everything that had happened.

"Something's going on here on this island, and I don't like it," he told her.

Emmy's grin disappeared. "I heard about the dead man. That, when combined with what happened to Dani . . . I can only imagine the stress that you're probably under right now."

"I just want to keep everyone safe."

"That's what you do best." There was no teasing in Emmy's voice, only sincerity. She shifted. "It looks like you and Dani are getting along pretty well."

Levi shook his head, needing to nip that rumor in the bud. "Only in a professional sense."

"She's a nice girl. Pretty too."

"Emmy..." Warning stained his voice.

She shrugged and took a step back, her glimmering eyes full of tease. "I'm just saying."

Only Emmy could get away with this conversation. Anyone else, and Levi might bite their head off at the mere suggestion that he could have room for anyone else in his life besides Adrienne.

"For all we know, Dani could be married," Levi finally said. "She could be in a serious relationship. We don't know any of those things. Besides, I would be crossing the line if I made a move on an amnesiac who was a part of one of my police investigations."

Emmy frowned and let out a breath. "When you say it that way..."

Levi nodded, glad that she'd seen his point. "Exactly."

"Then again, sometimes I think you can really see who someone is in a situation like this." Some of the apology disappeared from her gaze.

"What do you mean?" Levi stared at his sister, interested to see where she was going with this.

"I mean, when you strip away everything that defines us as people... maybe that's when you can see who someone really is at their core. Dani doesn't have a career or family or locale to paint a picture of her life. She only has the qualities that are knit into the fiber of her being. Without knowing anything about her—none of the titles people traditionally wear—it's clear that she's kind, generous, and helpful, to name a few things. It's kind of refreshing really."

"I always appreciate your perspective, Emmy." Levi spoke the truth. His sister was a free spirit. She saw life differently than almost anybody he'd ever met. Her perspective never failed to change Levi's outlook either—though he was slow to admit that to her on most occasions.

"And in the matter of romance, all of this will be behind us one day and then . . ." Emmy shrugged, making it clear she still thought Levi and Dani could have a future together.

Levi chuckled and shook his head. "You never give up, do you?"

"I'm just trying to look out for my older brother."

He tapped the tip of Emmy's pert nose with his finger. "How about you look out for yourself? I don't see any wedding ring on your finger—though I could name a couple of guys who'd happily put one there."

Emmy had always gotten a lot of attention from men, but she never seemed interested. She said when she met the perfect person, she'd know. There was no need to waste time with any others.

"There's nothing to look out for," Emmy said. "I'm living my best life, as they say. I don't need a ring for that."

"Well, there you go." Levi offered a definite nod. "It looks like we're both content. Just don't tell dad because he wants grandbabies from at least one of us one day."

Emmy let out a chuckle. "He's going to have to wait for quite a while on that one."

"I guess so." Levi took a step back. "I think that's enough heart-to-heart conversation for this evening. I've got to run. Colby is headed to Fire and Rescue in another hour or so. I asked him to keep an eye on this place tonight."

Emmy grinned. "Sounds good. Good night, big brother. I'll see you in the morning."

CHAPTER TWENTY-SEVEN

DANI GLANCED up from the table, where she ate bacon and eggs, when she heard somebody step into the inn.

Her heart skipped a beat when she spotted Levi standing by the front door wearing his customary cowboy boots, jeans, and a plaid shirt.

What was she doing? She had no business feeling excited when she saw Levi. Her heart shouldn't speed, her palms shouldn't sweat, and her breath definitely shouldn't catch.

It was a shame that Dani had to keep reminding herself of that.

Levi's boots clanked across the wooden floor until he reached the table. He paused and gave her a nod. There was a new look in his eyes—a look that seemed to indicate he had an update.

Dani braced herself for whatever that might be.

"Morning, Dani," Levi started.

"Good morning." Dani's throat burned as she said the words.

"How's it going, big bro?" Emmy paced to the table from the stove, another plate in her hands.

"It's going." He placed his hands atop of one of the chairs but made no move to sit down or join them.

"Why don't you eat with us?" Emmy held up the plate in her hands. "I have plenty of food."

"I wish I could, but I have a busy day ahead of me."

Emmy paused, as if sensing that something was wrong. "What's going on?"

He let out a long breath. "A couple of things. I'm getting all the Sanctuary Watchers together. We're going to go look for Skeeter."

"No one has seen him still?" Emmy stared at her brother, her eyes narrowing with concern.

Levi shook his head. "No, and it's been several days now. I'm getting worried about the foal. He shouldn't be separated from his mom this long."

Dani listened to the conversation with interest. She assumed Skeeter was a horse. But she also assumed that officers here wouldn't be able to put their eyes on every horse all the time. Their jobs fascinated her.

"Why does that worry you?" Dani finally asked.

"You think something happened to the horse? Skeeter is a horse, right?"

"He is. And it's always a possibility around here that one of our horses could be ill or injured. Basically, we just like to know all the horses are accounted for, especially the young ones."

"That makes sense." Dani knew the youngest and the oldest would be the most vulnerable of the population.

"As soon as I finish up here, I'll head out to help." Emmy set the plate on the table, suddenly looking as if she wanted to hurry up and eat.

"I'd love to help also, if you need me." Dani's words seemed to hang in the air, and she wondered if she was out of line in volunteering.

"It's probably best if you stay here." Levi shrugged almost apologetically.

"Why is that?" Dani stared at him, waiting for his answer. Why would it be better if she stayed here?

He hesitated again before saying, "I got a note this morning at the station. It was about you."

Her breath hitched. "And?"

"The author indicated that it would be in our best interest to put out a press release informing people a dead body washed ashore."

"A dead body? Are they talking about me?" Dani pointed to herself.

"That was my impression."

She shook her head. "Why would someone do that?"

"Maybe because they know if the wrong person finds out you're alive, that you'll be a target."

The blood drained from her face.

"Do you think that?" she finally asked.

Levi glanced around as if he wished he had some privacy. A second later, he continued, "You *were* shot. Right now, the person who pulled that trigger must think you're dead. If this person sees you out and about on the island, it could be a different story."

Dani's blood went cold. But Levi had a point. She could still be in danger.

She hated to think that was true. But she had to be smart about things also.

"Do you have any idea who left that note?" she finally asked.

"We don't. We have a security camera, but it was too dark outside for the images to be helpful."

"Are you going to send out a notice to the media about me?"

"I don't think it's a good idea, not until we have more details. Your safety is our first priority."

After a moment, Dani nodded. "I'll stay here then. Of course. But if at any time there's anything you need me to do . . . just let me know."

Levi offered another one of his curt nods. "I'll

do that." His gaze went back to Emmy, who'd already finished eating. "You think you can be at the Community Safety Headquarters building in five?"

Emmy looked at the dishes on the counter, as if trying to calculate how much time it would take to clean up.

"I've got the kitchen," Dani said. "It's the least that I can do."

"Are you sure?" Emmy pressed her lips together as if uncertain. "Your arm is in a sling..."

"I can figure it out. It might take longer than usual, but I can load a dishwasher and handwash a few pots and pans ... I think. You go find that horse."

More than anything, Dani wanted to be out there also. The thought of being confined to a house indefinitely wasn't appealing.

But she had no other choice right now.

It wasn't just herself that Dani could be putting in danger.

It was anyone around her.

And that wasn't okay.

AS LEVI and Nelly paused atop a sand dune, Levi removed his cowboy hat. He ran his hand through his hair, the heat getting to him more today than it usually did. Even though it was September, summerlike heat lingered today, and the thermometer climbed into the high eighties.

A group of fourteen people had been out searching for their foal, but Skeeter was nowhere to be seen.

That wasn't to say that the horse wasn't on the island. With eight thousand acres, it was almost impossible to cover every inch. Sometimes, the horses hunkered beneath the low-hanging branches of live oak trees to stay cool. If that was the case, their search would be even more difficult. The number of hiding spots on this island were uncountable.

Grant rode up on his horse and paused near Levi. "Anything?"

Levi stared at the peaceful ocean in the distance as he shook his head. "Nothing I've heard about. But I'm not ready to give up searching yet."

"I have a bad feeling in my gut about all of this."

Hearing the words out loud only confirmed to Levi that he wasn't off base with his feelings. "Me too."

"We'll keep looking. The Sanctuary Watchers feel very passionate about locating Skeeter. Especially Mary Lou." Grant paused. "Speaking of which, she's been looking for you."

Levi shook his head, fighting the grimace that wanted to spread across his face. "I'm sure she has."

Grant flashed a smile, making no attempt to hide the fact that he was egging Levi on. But his friend also knew better than to push any harder.

Instead, Grant cleared his throat. "By the way, the Fergusons came out and asked us what we were doing."

At even the mention of the family's name, Levi's back muscles tightened. "Is that right? What did you tell them?"

"Just that we were trying to locate some of our wild horses."

"And they said?"

"That we should consider putting them behind fences and that would solve a lot of our problems."

Levi clenched his teeth. "These horses were here long before we were. It seems unfair to them to confine them behind fences when they're used to being corralled only by the water."

"I think so too. But you know the Fergusons."

Levi remembered that conversation he had with Abigail Ferguson about Grant. Sometime, when the time was right, he would ask his friend more about that.

But not now.

Just then, Levi's phone beeped. He looked down and saw it was Agent Steve McConnell from the North Carolina State Bureau of Investigation.

He excused himself and put his phone to his ear. "Hey, Steve. What's going on?"

"I thought you would want to know that I had an ID on your John Doe."

Levi's breath hitched.

He couldn't wait to hear who this guy was.

CHAPTER TWENTY-EIGHT

DANI STOOD at the kitchen sink washing a pot when another memory hit her.

Or *tried* to hit her.

She pressed her soapy palms onto the countertop and closed her eyes. What was it? She feared the recollection would disappear before ever truly materializing.

Dani tried to even her breaths, tried to gain any type of control that she could. In and out. In and out.

Deep breath. And exhale.
Deep breath. And exhale.
Deep breath. And exhale.

The memory had just been a flash, really. But in the moment, Dani had remembered doing dishes. The location didn't strike her as a house. The sterile environment seemed too commercial.

Maybe it was a kitchen at an office?

That was her best guess.

She leaned harder into the kitchen counter, ignoring the moisture that dampened the edge of her shirt.

So maybe Dani had worked in an office. If that was true, it would mean she'd had coworkers. She desperately needed to remember. Even if she could recall her last name, so many of her questions would be answered.

Dani squeezed her eyes shut, praying for more memories to emerge. As the clean scent of soap floated around her, her mind drifted back to another time...

A man and woman smiled at her as they held a birthday cake with sparkling candles in their hands.

They sang to her while streamers hung in the background.

She was sixteen—at least according to the candles on the cake.

A sheet cake with white icing and teal-colored trim was placed on a table in front of her as the man and the woman glowed at her. Dani listened to the sounds of "Happy Birthday" as it faded and then she blew the candles out.

It must have been her birthday party.

Were that man and woman her parents? In her gut, Dani knew they were.

In her gut, she also knew that they weren't around anymore.

A moment of grief welled in her, even though Dani couldn't recall any details. But she felt certain that something tragic had happened to her mom and dad.

In her mind, she glanced around the table, looking for anyone else who might have eaten some cake with her. Nobody else there.

Was Dani an only child? If she was and if her parents were dead, that might explain why nobody was out looking for her.

But what about that other memory? The one of an office?

Maybe Dani had told people in the office she was going out of town for a while. No one would try to contact her if they thought she was on vacation or on a cruise.

She kept her eyes closed, still waiting for more memories to hit her.

But there was nothing else.

Dani prayed that more and more of these recollections would fill her. Maybe she'd slowly remember who she was.

She only hoped that she wasn't disappointed in the person she discovered.

TEN MINUTES LATER, Levi arrived at the Community Safety Headquarters building. The NCSBI had emailed him some information on their victim, and Levi wanted to print it out.

Dr. Knightly showed up just as Levi plucked the printouts from the printer and followed Levi to his desk.

"The victim's name is Paul Robinson," Levi told him, his eyes glued to the report. "He was thirty-three and lived up in the Norfolk, Virginia, area. Never married. No kids."

Levi hoped some of this information might offer some clues about what had happened.

Knightly stepped behind Levi to read the report over his shoulder. "It looks like he was a lawyer."

"So how did he end up here? Dead?"

Dr. Knightly shook his head. "Good question."

"I'll put in a few phone calls and see what I can find out."

"I know you're trying to keep this all under wraps. But I saw that some reporters showed up this morning to do an article on the search party looking for Skeeter."

Levi's gaze darkened. It was the first he'd heard about that. "I'm not sure how they caught wind of what was happening."

"You know they like to monitor our police scanners."

"That's why I try to keep as much off them as I can, just for that reason."

Dr. Knightly crossed his arms. "One of the watchers must have reported it then."

"I'm going to need to have a talk with them then. Privacy is everything in situations like this."

"I hope you find some answers." Dr. Knightly took a step back. "I know you're going to want to look into his background more and talk to any of his known associates."

"That's a definite."

But for now, Levi was going to start by talking with Dani.

CHAPTER TWENTY-NINE

DANI FELT UNREASONABLY nervous as Levi lowered himself across from her on the couch at the inn.

She knew he had something to tell her. But Dani had something to tell him also.

Levi started first. "Does the name Paul Robinson mean anything to you?"

She let the name settle in her mind then shook her head. "It doesn't ring any bells. Why?"

"He's the man who was found dead on the same night I found you."

Dani sucked in a shallow breath. "Is that right? Is there anything else you know about him that you can share? Maybe it will trigger something."

"Apparently, he was an attorney up in Norfolk."

She looked up at Levi and frowned. "I wish I

could help. I really do. But the name doesn't sound familiar, nor do I remember his face."

He nodded slowly. "That's what I thought, but I needed to ask."

"I understand." Dani licked her lips, trying to figure out how to broach the subject of her memories. She decided just to dive right in. "Another memory came back to me today."

Dani told him about the brief flashes from her past that had come to her.

When she finished, Levi nodded slowly. "Good. I'm glad that you're starting to remember. You just need to give it some time."

She nodded stiffly, wishing that time might speed up. But that was just wishful thinking.

"Did you find the foal?" she asked.

Levi pressed his lips together, his expression almost grim as he shook his head. "Unfortunately, we haven't. We're hoping that someone somewhere has seen something."

"I hope so too." Dani meant the words. Cape Corral was obviously special. She hated to think about anything happening to one of those horses.

"If you remember anything else, let me know, okay?"

Dani nodded. "Of course."

Levi stood. No doubt, he had to get back to work.

And Dani needed to get back to . . . nothing.

She hated the thought of that.

She needed to think of a way to keep herself busy or she might just lose her mind.

AS SOON AS Levi stepped outside the inn, his phone rang again. He hoped it might be an update on the foal.

Instead, he saw it was Kayla. He put the device to his ear. "Hey, Kayla. What's going on?"

"Are you nearby?"

"Just leaving Emmy's place."

"Perfect. I'm around the corner. Stay there for a minute. There's something you need to hear."

Levi put his phone away, hating the ominous sound in her tone. The woman was level-headed and not prone to drama. She obviously thought something was important if she was asking him to wait in the middle of this investigation.

The realtor appeared around the corner a moment later, wearing jean shorts and a tank top. She stepped onto the porch and into the shade before speaking. "Thanks for waiting, Levi. I like having conversations face-to-face much more than on the phone."

"Me too. What's going on?"

The corners of her lips tugged down in a frown. "I just got a notification that some paperwork has been filed. Remember that piece of land that I said this Wilhelmina Corporation would need to obtain in order to have an easement onto that property that they purchased?"

"I do."

"Well, I just found out that Ed Wilkes passed away."

"I'm sorry to hear that."

"I'm not sure who his next of kin is," Kayla continued. "But if that person happens to sell that land to Wilhelmina..."

Kayla didn't need to say anything else. Levi knew exactly what she was alluding to.

If this corporation got their hands on that land, then this island would never be the same. They couldn't let that happen.

"It gets worse," Kayla continued. "Someone has petitioned the county real estate board. This person is trying to zone that land for commercial use instead of residential."

"So they can build one of those big hotels there, I'm assuming." Levi's stomach clenched as he said the words.

"That's my guess."

Levi shook his head as his stomach continued to clench. "There's no way that the board should approve this."

Kayla's hazel gaze met his. "But you and I both know what it takes to get approval. Sometimes a little bit of cash under the table can push decisions in certain directions."

He didn't like the sound of that. "You think that board members could be paid off?"

She shrugged. "I hate to say it. But yes, I do. I have no proof, of course. Just a gut feeling."

Levi gritted his teeth.

It looked like his day had just gotten even busier.

CHAPTER THIRTY

"I THOUGHT you said she was dead."

Bobby felt the blood drain from him as he stared at the photo in front of him. An online article had come out this afternoon. In it, he could see a crowd gathered on Cape Corral.

He scanned the faces there. Most of the people, he didn't recognize. But there, peering out the window of a house, was a woman who looked vaguely familiar.

A woman who looked like Dani.

Bobby sucked in a quick breath.

"Do you care to explain yourself?" the Captain demanded.

Bobby looked up at his boss and felt a cold tremor rush through him. This wasn't supposed to happen.

He glanced at Ace beside him, and the two

shrugged. They both were indebted to the Captain, but Ace had just been brought on. He was already in just as deep as Bobby, though.

"I promise, I thought she was dead," Bobby insisted.

The Captain's eyes narrowed with impatience. "And where did you get that information? I thought you'd confirmed it with your own eyes."

"I asked around," Bobby rushed. "People said a body washed up. They made it sound like she was dead."

"Apparently, she isn't. I trusted you to take care of this." The Captain's voice turned to a low growl.

Another surge of panic rushed through him. "I promise. I can handle this. It's not too late. I can make things right."

"I'm afraid it is too late."

What did that mean? Did Bobby even want to know?

He had to convince his boss that he was on his side. "No, I'm in for whatever you want."

"You already had that opportunity and you failed." The Captain reached into his desk and pulled something out.

A gun.

Bobby's throat went dry. "I'll make it right. Just give me another chance."

"We've worked together for a while now,

haven't we, Bobby?" His boss stood and moved around his desk until he stood beside Bobby.

Sweat scattered across Bobby's forehead as he stared at the gun. "Yes, we have. You know how much this job means to me."

"Doesn't seem like it means enough to you."

He heard the warning in his boss's voice. He was *not* happy—and that was never a good thing. "It means everything to me."

"If I can't trust my men to tell me the truth, then I can't trust them at all."

"No, you've got to understand—"

Before Bobby could finish the statement, he heard the muted sound of a bullet rushing through the air.

He waited for the pain that he was sure to come.

He felt nothing.

Not yet.

But it wasn't too late.

Then he heard a gurgle beside him.

He swung his gaze toward Ace. His friend grasped his chest as blood gushed from it.

"Ace!" Bobby reached for his friend.

"Leave him alone!"

Bobby turned back toward the Captain and saw that the gun was pointed at him this time.

"That's where you were supposed to have shot Dani," the Captain barked.

Bobby opened his mouth, still determined to defend himself.

Instead, he heard the squeal coming from Ace.

His lung had been hit, hadn't it? His friend's face turned blue.

He was dying...

"Let me help him." Bobby looked up at the Captain, pleading with him.

"It's too late."

Just as he said the words, Ace collapsed onto the floor beside him.

Panic rushed through Bobby. Had that just happened?

"Your little boy is next," the Captain warned. "Finish the job. Or else."

I'm sorry, Dani. Bobby thought again.

He had no choice but to really kill her this time. No mistakes. No accidents.

Just cold-blooded murder.

That meant he needed to go back to Cape Coral and track her down. He'd come up with a cover story. He'd ask questions.

Then he'd figure out a plan.

CHAPTER THIRTY-ONE

DANI FELT an unusual amount of anxiety as she heard the commotion downstairs.

Maybe *commotion* was too strong a word. But their new guest had arrived to check in. Dani had already gotten rather comfortable at the inn with just her and Emmy being here. Knowing someone else would be staying made her surprisingly nervous.

The only thing that comforted her was the scent of chicken and biscuits that floated upstairs from the kitchen. The savory scent was somehow soothing.

She walked to the top of the steps and peered down, watching as Emmy greeted the newcomer.

It was a man. Probably in his thirties. He had dark hair and a big smile. Nothing about him screamed criminal.

But it was hard to know whom to trust in times like these.

"So what brings you to the island?" Emmy asked as they stood downstairs.

"I've always wanted to visit," the man said. "I am so glad that I finally have the opportunity to."

"Well, that's great," Emmy said. "We're happy to have you here in Cape Corral. Let me show you to your room."

Dani stepped back before Emmy or her guest could notice her listening to the conversation. She slipped into her room, and, as the pair finished mounting the stairs, stepped from her doorway.

Emmy grinned. "This is our other guest, Dani. Dani, this is William."

Dani nodded his way. "Nice to meet you."

He flashed a big grin back at her. "You as well."

Emmy opened the door on the opposite side of the hallway. "If you just want to leave your things in your room, I'm serving dinner in a few minutes. You're welcome to join us."

"I don't want you to have to worry about me," the man said. "I'll just grab something at one of the restaurants here."

Emmy chuckled. "The only restaurant in town is closed on Tuesdays. Sorry. It's my cooking or nothing."

"I guess your cooking will be fine then. Thank you."

Emmy turned back to Dani. "You'll be joining us too?"

Dani nodded, feeling another quell of nerves hit her. "That sounds great."

She was going to relax and behave like a normal person. There was nothing to be nervous about.

She only wished she didn't have to keep reminding herself of that fact.

LEVI SAW the picture in the online newspaper and felt his jaw clench.

This article, though it was short, had been written in what appeared to be record time. But that wasn't what concerned him.

How had that reporter managed to get a picture with Dani in it? Was this even legal?

Levi knew it was. The photo was a group shot. No names had been called out.

But if someone looked closely in the window at the inn, Dani was clearly visible.

If somebody was looking for her—the good guys or the bad guys—then this might be their opportunity to find her.

Levi closed his eyes for a moment. What was done was done. There was no taking this photo back.

But he had to be proactive now when it came to keeping Dani safe and protected, especially until she regained her memory. The last thing Levi wanted was for her to trust the wrong person.

He put his hat back on and strode to the door of his place.

Emmy had invited him over to eat tonight, and he wasn't going to turn down a meal.

Emmy was not only hospitable, but she'd learned to cook from their grandmother. She could make Southern dishes along with the best of them. Chicken and dumplings, collard greens, brisket. She made the best potato salad ever too.

But Levi had to admit he was also intrigued with the idea of seeing Dani again. He wanted to know if she'd remembered anything else.

Was the curiosity purely professional? He wanted to say yes. But another part of him was curious about the woman's past and what had made her into the person she was today.

Was that why Levi had put on some cologne right before he left his house?

He'd never admit it.

Instead, he hopped into his Jeep and took off toward his sister's place.

Maybe having a break from the investigation would be good for him. Maybe it would allow him relax and think more clearly.

That was his excuse, at least.

CHAPTER THIRTY-TWO

AS SOON AS Dani saw Levi walk through the front door, some of the tension left her shoulders. She hadn't even realized she was so apprehensive, but she obviously was.

Even though Emmy's food was delicious, Dani had only picked at it. Emmy had served oven-baked barbecue chicken with rice, gravy, green beans, and homemade biscuits. Everything looked delicious, and Dani wished she had more of an appetite so she could enjoy it.

Emmy sat across from Dani, and William sat beside her. Colby had also joined them, sitting next to Emmy, and he made it no secret how much he was enjoying the meal.

But, right now, Dani's gaze was only on Levi as he strode across the room and paused near her. "How's everybody doing today?"

He spoke as if he owned the place. Dani supposed that was a good quality when you were the chief law enforcement officer on the island. A shrinking violet wouldn't have the same effect.

Introductions were exchanged before Levi took a seat at the head of the table.

Dani noticed the way he observed the man beside her. Levi was sizing William up, wasn't he? Was that the whole reason Levi had come to eat with them?

"So what brings you to the island?" Levi asked the man.

William lowered his fork. "Always wanted to see the place."

"You won't be disappointed," Levi said. "It's beautiful here in Cape Corral."

"Yes, it is. I'm hoping to do some off-roading and see the wild horses. I even brought a fishing pole."

"Sounds like a great vacation," Levi told him.

The rest of the conversation at dinner was pleasant and casual. If Dani let herself, she might even forget all her problems for a moment.

As soon as they finished eating, Levi turned to her. "Could I speak with you?"

"Of course." Dani stood and placed her napkin on the table. A thrill of excitement went through her at the thought of speaking with him alone. But first, she turned to Emmy. "I can help you clean this up in a moment."

"Don't be silly." Emmy waved her off. "I've got it. Better yet, Colby's got it."

"I didn't tell you I had to eat and run?" Colby flashed a smile before the two of them started teasing each other again.

With a reluctant nod, Dani followed Levi out to the back porch. They sat on some old glider rockers and stared at the woods—and the old, crooked tombstones in front of the trees. Dani tried to make out some of the names, but it was no use.

The sun had set, leaving the whole island dark again. It didn't feel quite as scary when Levi was here with her. Dani couldn't help but wonder what he wanted to talk about. She had a feeling it was important.

"Dani, I just wanted to let you know that an article ran today in the paper about our missing foal." Levi rubbed his hand against his jeans as his gaze met hers.

Dani nodded, unsure where he was going with this. "That's good, right?"

He shrugged and twisted his head, making it clear something was wrong. "In most cases, I suppose it would be. But in this case, not so much."

"I don't understand what you're getting at." And why was he telling her this? Though she cared about the foal and hoped it was found, this issue hardly concerned her.

Levi pulled out his phone and showed her a photo there. "If you look in the window of the inn, you can see that you're peering outside."

He handed her the phone, and Dani blew up the image. She sucked in a breath when she realized his words were true. She was clearly there in the photo if anyone looked closely enough.

Dani had peeked outside, just for a moment, to see what was going on. That must have been when the reporter took this picture. She'd had no idea.

Her heart pounded harder. "I don't know what to say. I didn't even see anybody with a camera and—"

"I'm not blaming you." Levi patted the air with his hands, as if urging her thoughts to slow. "I just wanted to give you a heads-up. If the person who shot you was shooting to kill and then he saw this picture..."

"Then he might come back to finish what he started." Dani felt the frown tugging at her lips.

"I'm sorry." Levi glanced at her, wearing a matching frown. "I know that's not what you want to hear."

She leaned back in the chair, suddenly craving a big, warm blanket she could wrap herself in, something that would make her feel secure and safe—even if she wasn't. "I just want to remember," she admitted. "If my brain was working like it should, we wouldn't have these problems. I could tell you who shot me and what happened. Then I could return home and get out of your hair."

"No one here thinks that you're in their hair, so to speak," Levi reassured her. "But I know it must be disconcerting for you to be here alone."

She nodded slowly, an unseen weight pressing on her shoulders. "If I think about it too much, I start to feel a bit panicked. It's like I don't know what my place in this world is."

"Just know you have a place here until you get it all figured out."

Levi's words sent a burst of warmth through her. Dani touched her throat as she felt a burn start there. "Thank you. I can't tell you how much I appreciate that."

Levi didn't say anything. Instead, he sat in silence—in a surprisingly comfortable silence. It was almost as if he wasn't in a hurry to leave.

Dani wasn't in a hurry for Levi to go either.

He was her security blanket, she realized. Whenever he was around, she felt safe.

And feeling safe wasn't underrated. Not by any stretch of the imagination.

LEVI SENSED that Dani didn't need to be alone right now. Besides, Emmy's back porch was inviting.

The front porch beckoned conversations with neighbors and passersby. The back porch invited solitude and more intimate conversations. The only thing that would make this better was if he could sit beside Dani. Put his arm around her as they listened to the crickets sing and the frogs play their symphony.

Dani suddenly sat up straight and pointed to something in the distance. "Did you see that?"

Levi instantly went on guard, one of his hands reaching to the holster where he kept his gun. "See what?"

His gaze scanned the woods, but he didn't see any signs of trouble.

"There it is again." Dani pointed to the woods again.

As he followed her gaze, Levi's shoulders slumped and he let out a little laugh.

In the distance, barely visible in the dim light, a cat popped his head out of the brush. On the other side of him, another cat did the same thing.

"It's just a cat," he murmured.

"There must be at least six cats out here."

"We have quite the feral colony living in those woods."

Dani's head jerked toward him. "Really?"

"Don't worry. Emmy always puts food out for them. Our island veterinarian, Acadia, also comes to check on them. Twice a year, we capture them so they can be examined. If you see a cat with a nick on his ear, that means he's been fixed."

"I see." Dani's gaze remained on the felines. "They're actually kind of cute."

Levi watched the cats again. Their heads kept popping up at random places in the brush. He supposed if he let his mind go there, he could see how somebody would think they were intriguing.

"You guys have all kinds of wild creatures on this island, don't you?" Dani asked.

"We do. I guess it's just something else that makes this place feel a little bit exotic and a little bit like home."

"You're lucky to live here."

Levi shrugged and his jaw tightened for a moment before quickly loosening again. "When I was a kid, I thought all I wanted to do was leave. But then I left, and I realized everything I loved was here. So I came back."

What wasn't he saying? It didn't matter. It wasn't any of Dani's business. "It must be nice to have roots."

"It's sometimes overwhelming." Levi let out a quick chuckle that almost sounded more like a grunt. "I only say that because I have aunts and uncles and cousins living here in this place. Everybody always knows everything that's going on, it seems."

A smile fluttered across Dani's face. "That actually sounds kind of nice."

Levi glanced over at her. He'd heard the longing in her voice. It had to be hard not knowing where she belonged.

But he'd meant it when he said Dani had a place here for as long as she needed. She might think she was an inconvenience, but Levi didn't see it that way.

In the short time since he'd found Dani, she had been a nice addition to the island. Levi had always admired people with good work ethics and kind hearts. Dani seemed to fit the bill for both of those.

Maybe if circumstances were different, he *would* want to get to know Dani a little bit better. But they weren't different, so getting too close right now wasn't a good idea.

Just then, he heard another noise in the woods.

This one sounded too big to be a cat. A horse maybe? With the thick underbrush, the wild horses didn't generally like to come this way. Every once in a while, the herd had a rebel, though.

Dani tensed beside him, leaning forward in her chair.

"Levi...?"

"Why don't you go back inside for a minute?" Levi suggested.

Dani looked up at him, her eyes quivering with fear. But she didn't ask any questions. Instead, she rose and stepped toward the door.

But before she could even reach it, a bullet sliced through the air.

CHAPTER THIRTY-THREE

DANI FELT her feet lift into the air as Levi scooped her into his arms. In the blink of an eye, he whisked her away. The next instant, she was inside the inn and the door closed behind Levi as he went to investigate.

Her heart pounded in her ribcage as images barraged her.

Her hands went to her head as it began to pulse uncontrollably.

Everything around her disappeared.

Until Emmy's voice pulled her out of it. "Dani? What's wrong? What happened?"

The sound of another bullet pierced the air outside.

Emmy gasped. "Come on. Let's get you away from this wall."

She gripped Dani's arm and led her away just as Colby appeared from the living room.

"Is that gunfire?" he rushed.

"Does Minnie's cake have twelve layers?"

"What?" Colby paused.

"Yes. Yes! It was gunfire," Emmy rushed. "Can't I ever be clever around you?"

"I don't know what that means, but I'm going to give Levi a hand." Colby rushed toward the back door.

"Be careful!" Emmy called, all teasing gone.

Before she could get her thoughts straight, Dani sat on the edge of Emmy's bed, and Emmy bent toward her.

"Did you see who was shooting?"

Dani tried to concentrate, but all she could think about was the sound of those bullets. A deep buried memory desperately tried to form. But something blocked it.

"Did you see who was doing this?" Emmy repeated.

Dani shook her head, still barely with it. "The shots came out of nowhere."

"Is Levi okay?"

She nodded. "He got me inside and went after the gunman."

Emmy frowned, moving to sit beside Dani on the bed. "I thought it would be safer in here. Just in case."

Dani squeezed her eyes shut, realizing that the memory wasn't going to materialize. No matter how much she willed that to happen, it wasn't going to be the case.

"Where's your guest?" Sudden panic rushed through Dani.

"He went out for a walk right after dinner," Emmy said. "Hopefully, he's far away from here by now."

Dani hoped Emmy's assessment was correct.

But for now, all they could do was wait.

And Dani prayed for the best.

That's right, she prayed. Somehow, without knowing the details of her past, she knew that praying was important to her. She knew that God was real. That He was there.

And she knew that they all needed Him more right now than they ever had before.

LEVI DUCKED BEHIND A TREE, holding his gun in his hand.

There were disadvantages to the darkness outside. For starters, he couldn't see a thing in these thick woods.

But he knew that the gunman was out there. Somewhere. Not too far away, but close enough to make the shot. A bad shot, but a shot nonetheless.

If that gun had been fired by someone who knew what they were doing, Dani would be dead right now.

Was this the same person who'd tried to kill her earlier?

That was the only thing that made sense. Someone must have seen that photo. If it had come out in the newspaper around three o'clock, that would give somebody approximately five hours to get here. They could have come down from Virginia or come up from the Outer Banks.

He'd have to think about that later.

Right now, Levi wanted to concentrate on finding the person responsible.

In the distance, he heard someone moving through the foliage.

Running footsteps.

The shooter was attempting to escape.

Levi couldn't let that happen.

Still holding his gun, he took off through the thick maritime forest.

He dodged trees and branches and underbrush.

He couldn't let this guy get away. Too much was at stake.

Levi continued to push himself.

Finally, he paused.

The best thing he could do right now was to listen. He hadn't heard the man moving in a while.

Had the guy turned? Or was this man hunkering down, preparing for a surprise attack?

He didn't know. But he wanted to figure it out.

Silence hung around him except for the sound of crickets and a slight rustling of leaves in the wind.

The skin on the back of his neck began to rise.

Levi knew what that meant.

The gunman was watching him right now, wasn't he?

He was being stalked like prey during hunting season.

Levi needed to plan his next step very carefully —if he wanted to survive.

CHAPTER THIRTY-FOUR

LEVI TURNED as he heard a footstep. He aimed his gun, ready to pull the trigger.

Before he could, a familiar face appeared in front of him.

Colby.

Levi released his breath and lowered his gun.

Colby raised his hands in submission. "It's just me. I thought you could use some help."

Levi knew his friend just wanted to help, but his timing couldn't be worse. He put his finger over his lips, indicating that Colby should be quiet.

Levi said nothing, listening for any signs of where the shooter had gone.

Everything was quiet around them.

A moment later, Levi frowned and shook his head. "I lost his trail. But he can't be that far away."

"Do you want to divide up and look for him?"

They could cover more ground that way . . . "Let's do that. But be careful. It's too dark to see well, and this man could be anywhere."

Colby nodded, and they both went different ways.

Levi moved carefully through the forest, not only on the lookout for a gunman, but for other wild creatures that liked to roam this island.

Fifteen minutes later, Levi hadn't found anybody. Nor had Colby.

This gunman was long gone.

He must have slipped away while Levi was distracted and talking to Colby. It was the only thing that made sense.

Levi chomped down, resisting the urge to grit his teeth. They'd been so close to finding this guy. To finding answers.

But now they were back at square one.

Colby holstered his gun. "Any idea who it was?"

"I can only guess it was the same person who shot Dani before her body washed up on the beach."

Colby shook his head, his jaw tight. "How did he find her again?"

Levi explained the article with Dani's picture that had run in the newspaper.

Colby frowned. "That's unfortunate."

"Tell me about it. Did you see Dani inside? Was she okay?"

Colby nodded. "She was fine. Shaking but okay."

"What about Emmy? And her guest for the evening—William?"

"Emmy was fine. But her guest went out for a walk about five minutes before all this happened."

Levi's muscles tightened. Was that right? Maybe this guest wasn't who he had said he was.

Either way, Levi needed to find out for himself.

DANI AND EMMY both sprang from the bed as soon as they heard the front door open. They rushed toward the living room in time to see Levi and Colby step inside.

"Anything?" Emmy stepped closer to Colby.

Levi shook his head, his expression tight and grim. "He got away."

"Any idea who he is?" Dani asked.

"No, we didn't see him."

"Was it a hunter out past hours?" Emmy continued.

Dani's gaze went to Levi, and she studied his expression, looking for the truth. He stiffly shook his head. "I don't think so. I think it was someone aiming at Dani."

Dani's lungs froze as the statement hung in the air. She'd known that was the truth before Levi even said anything. But hearing the words out loud made the realization feel more real.

That memory tried to surface again, tried to push its way to the top of her thoughts. Dani squeezed her eyes shut, trying to let it come to life.

But it was no use. The memory seemed to be stuck in another dimension, and nothing that she did would help to produce it again.

When she opened her eyes, Levi stood in front of her, his gaze full of worry and concern. "Are you hanging in?"

Dani nodded, but she wasn't sure the action was all that convincing. "Just shaken."

"As anybody would be." He stepped back and glanced at Emmy. "We need to go find your guest."

"You think William could be behind this?" Dani asked.

"I'm trying not to jump to any conclusions. But his timing is suspicious." Levi turned toward Emmy. "When exactly did William book his stay here?"

"This afternoon." Emmy shrugged. "But that's not entirely unusual."

"His timing couldn't have been worse." Levi rubbed his jaw. "That's when that article came out."

Emmy pulled her arms across her chest and nodded. "I suppose you're right."

"Colby, will you stay here while I look for him?"

"Of course. Whatever I can do."

As Dani watched Levi leave, she began praying again. She really hoped she hadn't brought trouble with her to this island. But it was beginning to look more and more like she had.

CHAPTER THIRTY-FIVE

LEVI HAD DRIVEN for only five minutes when he saw a shadow walking down the sandy road. He pulled the Jeep over and threw it in Park before hopping out.

Sure enough, William appeared in the beam of his headlights a moment later.

"Can I help you?" The man raised his hand against the glare of the high beams.

Levi observed him for a moment. The man didn't appear to have a gun on him, nor did he look winded or like he'd been running through the woods.

If William had been in the woods on the other side of Emmy's house, it would have taken the man at least fifteen minutes to walk back to this side of the island. Levi estimated that only about ten minutes had passed.

But he wasn't letting the guy off the hook this easily.

"We're investigating a shooting," Levi started. "Can you tell me where you've been since you left the inn?"

"A shooting?" The man's eyes widened. "In a place like this?"

Levi nodded and waited for the man's response.

After a couple of seconds, he shook his head and continued, "I just walked down the street to stretch my legs for bit. It's been a long day of traveling with lots of sitting, and I thought I could use the exercise." William paused and tilted his head. "Is everything okay?"

"Considering we have a gunman here on the island, I'd say no," Levi said. "Did you see anything suspicious while you were out?"

"No." William raised his shoulders before dropping them quickly. "It was peaceful and quiet. I thought I heard something in the distance, but I assumed that maybe it was fireworks or someone doing some target practice."

Levi stared at the man a moment. He had no reason to suspect William wasn't telling the truth. Going around making accusations at visitors definitely wasn't the way Levi wanted to do his job. Yet he had to remain cautious.

His only comfort right now was in knowing that he'd left Colby at the inn to keep an eye on

Emmy and Dani. He knew Colby would protect them with his life.

Instead, Levi had called Grant to come and help him search. That way he could keep things official.

"Thank you for your cooperation," Levi finally said. "You should get inside until the shooter is caught."

William nodded. "I'll do that. Good luck finding this guy."

As the man continued down the road, Levi recognized Grant's truck ahead. As he flagged his friend down, he made a quick call to Emmy. He told her he was okay, that William was on his way back, and to hunker down until he returned.

"Anything?" Grant asked as he rolled down his window.

"My number one suspect appears to be innocent."

"So someone actually shot at our mystery woman?" Grant repeated.

"That's how it looks. The gunman didn't appear to be aiming at me."

Grant clucked his tongue. "I don't like what I'm hearing."

"Believe me, none of us do."

"Do you want to keep looking?"

Levi let out a sigh as he thought about their next steps. "Let's patrol the island a bit longer and make sure nothing is amiss. But I have a feeling that whoever the shooter was, he's long gone by now. I'm going to head down to the docks to see if we've had any boats pull up anytime recently."

"So many people have docks on their property that it will be impossible to see everybody who's coming and going."

Levi knew his friend's words were true. But he wouldn't forgive himself unless he checked the area out, just to be safe.

He would do anything he could to protect the people here.

And he now considered Dani one of them.

DANI SAT on the couch trying to sip a warm cup of tea. But the drink seemed tasteless. Every time she raised her cup, she noticed how badly her hands trembled.

William had arrived back at the inn and slipped upstairs to his room. Emmy and Colby had escaped into the kitchen to talk between themselves for a moment. She heard them murmuring to each other about something—probably the shooter. Did they think he was connected with Dani? Was that because he was?

Either way, Dani welcomed the moment of

quiet. She leaned her head against the couch and took a deep breath, hoping her pulse would slow.

As she closed her eyes, memories tried to hit her again.

She didn't attempt to stop them.

Instead, in an instant, she was transported from Cape Corral.

She was . . . out at sea. On a midsize boat. Standing near the railing.

A man with a blurred face stood in front of her.

Dani squinted, trying to make out his features.

It was no use. She couldn't bring the man into focus.

"I'm sorry, Dani," he said.

The next instant, the sound of a bullet exploded in the air.

Pain burst through Dani, then water imprisoned her.

Panic clawed at her. "Help!"

She had to get help if she wanted to survive. Otherwise, the ocean would be her grave.

But as a dark wave overtook her, she felt herself fading . . .

"Dani? Are you okay?" someone said.

Dani's eyes flew open. Emmy stood in front of her.

Dani sat up straight, trying to even out her breathing. As she glanced at the wooden floor, she realized she'd dropped her cup. The porcelain had shattered into uncountable pieces.

And she hadn't even noticed it happen.

"I'm so sorry." Dani reached down to pick up a piece. As she did, a sharp corner caught her finger. Blood appeared, and she sucked in a breath.

"What happened?" a deep voice said. "Is everyone okay?"

Dani looked toward the door in time to see Levi step in. In two seconds flat, he was by her side and holding her hand.

"I was just clumsy," Dani muttered.

"Let's get this cleaned up."

Levi kept his hand in hers as he led her into the kitchen and started some water at the sink. Dani held her finger beneath the spray, letting the water do its job. How had she slipped into the memory so quickly? And what had those images meant?

"Nothing happened?" Levi questioned, looking down at her.

Dani had to admit that something about his closeness right now got her heart pounding. She scolded herself for feeling that way, but the reprimand did nothing to stop her racing heart. "I had a flashback. I didn't even realize what was happening or that I dropped the cup."

"What did you see, Dani?" Levi turned to face her fully, staring deeply into her eyes with that intelligent gaze of his.

The water still ran over her hand, but she hardly noticed it. All her attention was on Levi and his question.

Dani's voice trembled as she tried to speak. She cleared her throat, willing herself to find her inner strength. It was no use. Bad memories, the flashbacks, the trauma—they all seized her right now, and she felt helpless to stop them.

Levi turned off the water and grabbed a paper towel. He pressed it over her finger and then turned back toward her, not backing down. He wouldn't until he had answers.

"I saw an image of myself on a boat at night. Someone apologized to me before shooting me and watching as I fell into the water."

"What did this person look like?"

Dani shook her head a little too quickly and shrugged. The motion made her feel off balance, and she had to prop her hip against the counter. Levi kept his hand on hers, still pressing that paper towel into her finger. It didn't matter that blood had seeped through all of the layers. He simply folded it again and pressed it harder.

"I tried to make out what he looked like," Dani started. "But it was no use. His face was just a blob of darkness."

"That's probably normal in situations like this," Levi said. "Your mind is trying to block out all the bad memories. It's trying to protect you."

"Which is strange because I think the best way to protect myself right now is to identify this man." Her voice cracked.

Levi looked over her shoulder at Emmy and Colby, who stood in the space between the kitchen and living room. "Did your guest get back here?"

Emmy nodded. "He did. He went up to his room. Said he was tired. Is everything okay?"

"I don't think he's the shooter," Levi said. "If he was, he's a great actor. He showed no signs of exertion."

"So you think the man who shot me might still be here on the island?" Dani's voice trembled again.

"I think that gunman is connected with you. I have a feeling he's going to remain on this island. He doesn't want you alive for some reason. Maybe you know something. Either way, the situation is deadly, to say the least."

Dani's head throbbed harder. "Then what am I going to do?"

"I'm going to sleep on the couch here tonight just to keep an eye on things. Then in the morning, we'll come up with a new plan."

CHAPTER THIRTY-SIX

LEVI HARDLY SLEPT ALL NIGHT. How could he with everything that was going on? Every time he heard a squeak or the wind blow, he sat up straight on the couch and waited for more trouble to come.

But the night had been uneventful.

The good news was that Dani seemed to be regaining more of her memories. Maybe with some time, she could remember exactly what had happened to her.

Levi had just stood from the couch and folded his blanket when he heard footsteps coming down the stairs. They sounded too heavy to be Dani. When William appeared, Levi wasn't surprised.

The man was already wearing a khaki-colored vest and a floppy hat.

"Morning." William's voice wasn't quite as friendly as it had been when the two had first met.

"Looks like you're ready for the day." Levi made every effort to keep his voice professional and non-accusatory.

William shrugged. "I chartered a fishing boat, so I'm going to get out there and see what I can catch."

"Emmy usually fixes breakfast for her guests."

"No worries. I told her yesterday that I wouldn't be here."

Was that because Levi had scared the man away? Levi didn't know that answer. "I hope you have a great trip and that you catch some big ones."

"Thanks. I'm hoping for that also."

With one more nod at Levi, William stepped to the door and disappeared outside.

Levi let out the breath he hadn't realized he was holding. He supposed that the man's presence here made Levi more tense than he wanted to admit. He'd feel better knowing that William was out of the house.

A few minutes later, Emmy's bedroom door opened, and she stepped out. She frowned as she paced toward Levi.

"I need to go down to Nags Head," she said. "I have a dentist appointment. You know how much I love clean teeth."

Yes, while most people hated the dentist, Emmy loved going. But that was the least of Levi's concerns right now. "What about Dani?"

Emmy shrugged. "She could go with me."

Levi didn't like the thought of that. Too many things could go wrong.

"She can hang out with me today," Levi said.

Emmy tilted her head. "I'm sure you have a lot to do. Maybe I could just send someone else—"

"Don't be ridiculous. Dani is more than welcome to ride around with me. It probably won't be as much fun for her, but at least I can keep an eye on her."

Emmy nodded and glanced at her watch. "Since my guest doesn't want breakfast, I thought I'd leave a note for Dani that she could help herself to whatever she wants. I'd rather get going now while I can."

"Understood. Have a safe trip. Is Colby going with you?"

"That's the plan. He needs to stop by the hardware store."

Now Levi just needed to wait for Dani to wake up so he could explain to her the schedule for the day.

DANI COULDN'T HELP but think that Levi was babysitting her as she sat beside him in the Jeep. They patrolled the island, on the lookout for various horses or any sign of trouble.

Levi seemed distracted. No doubt his thoughts were on many things.

"Any more memories resurface?"

Dani looked out the window, letting the fresh breeze hit her face. "No, nothing new. I was hoping something might be stirred up last night as I was sleeping, but there wasn't anything there. I'm sorry."

"Don't apologize. I'm just trying to make sense of things myself."

Making sense of things seemed like an impossible task. That's all she'd been trying to do as well.

They rode for a few more minutes in silence. Finally, Dani cleared her throat. "So, is this a job that you can see yourself doing for a long time?"

One of Levi's hands casually gripped the steering wheel as they bounced along the road. But she saw his jaw tighten. The action was so slight that most people would have missed it.

Dani hadn't.

"I have come to think of these horses almost as part of my family," Levi said. "Someone has to look out for them too. I figured this was the job that God gave me."

"I feel like there's a but in there."

He cast her a quick glance. "Not really."

Dani nodded, accepting his answer. "Well, it seems like everybody needs someone to look out for them. I'm sure these horses would express their appreciation for all your hard work if they could."

"It's funny how each of them has its own personality."

Dani pointed at one in the distance. "Why is that one by himself?"

"That's Rocky. He's a lone stallion."

"And what does that mean?" Was Levi simply waxing poetic about the horses?

"It means that he is getting older and no longer has a harem to accompany him. Once that happens, the stallions normally go out on their own to live the rest of their lives in solitude."

Dani's heart squeezed at the imagery. "That seems sad."

"Maybe. But it's just what nature dictates."

Dani understood. Lately, she felt a bit like a lone stallion. Like everybody else had their groups, but she was standing out there alone. Not that anybody on the island had made her feel that way.

But since she couldn't remember her past . . . and since no one had stepped forward to say that she was missing . . . it had been a real eye-opener.

Dani wouldn't wish this feeling of loneliness on her worst enemy.

Just then, a truck blew by, horn pounding as the driver waved at Levi.

Dani glanced at Levi and saw his eyes narrow. "What was that about?"

His scowl deepened as he watched the truck in his rearview mirror.

"Everything okay?" she asked when Levi didn't offer an explanation.

"That was Johnny Ferguson. His family and the rest of the island seem to constantly be in a state of feuding."

Dani crossed her arms. "I'm sorry to hear that. I suppose, even in paradise, there can be troublesome times."

Levi rubbed his jaw. "You can say that again."

CHAPTER THIRTY-SEVEN

LEVI SLOWED as he crested the dune. He was by the North Banks, otherwise known as Ferguson territory. When it came to law enforcement, he couldn't have any biases. That meant he had to protect and watch out for the very people who ridiculed and scolded him.

But that wasn't what he was thinking about right now.

No, instead it was the expensive Land Rover that sat on an empty piece of property in the distance.

The very property Kayla had told him had been put under contract recently.

It was time Levi introduced himself to the people buying up land on the island.

He took a sharp turn and headed toward the Land Rover.

Levi sensed Dani watching him with questions in her eyes. He'd have to explain later.

Just yesterday, if Dani had been with him, he wouldn't take this chance. But now that her picture was public, there was no need to keep her hidden away. But there *was* an even greater need to keep an eye on her.

They bounced across the sand until Levi finally pulled off on a sandy patch and threw the Jeep in Park.

He glanced at Dani. "It's better if you wait here."

She stared ahead at the men standing outside the Land Rover and nodded. "Okay."

Levi climbed out and strode across the ground toward the people in the distance.

Three men were there, each dressed in expensive looking clothes—moisture-wicking polos, name-brand shorts, leather boat shoes.

They paused their conversation when they saw him.

"Can I help you?" one of them called. The man was older, maybe in his sixties, with gray hair and a neat mustache. He seemed like the type who'd be more comfortable on the golf course than at the beach. Every word, every action seemed refined.

"I'm Officer Levi Sutherland." He showed them the badge on his belt. "I like to keep an eye on things going on around here, and I've never seen you guys here before."

One of the men—the one who'd spoken just moments earlier—extended his hand. "Warren Wilhelmina. I just put a contract on this land."

That was exactly what Levi was afraid of. "Congratulations on the purchase."

The man nodded. "Thanks. We're excited to be here."

"You plan on building a second home on this property?"

Warren shrugged, his gaze aloof. "Eventually. I just wanted to get in on this island before all the land was bought up."

Levi's gaze traveled behind the man to his two other companions.

"Forgive me for being rude. These are my business associates, Mark and Calvin." Warren extended a hand in their direction.

Levi offered a curt nod as the men glanced up.

"I'm staying with my friend Thomas Ferguson right now. Maybe you know him?" Warren stared Levi down.

"Who doesn't?" Levi tried to keep his voice even. "Did you just get into town?"

"Just this morning by boat—since the road is washed out. I'm borrowing one of Tom's vehicles in the meantime."

"That's awfully nice of him. You going to be staying long?"

"Maybe a couple of days." Warren raised his chin, his eyes narrowing. "What's with the third degree?"

"No third degree. Like I said, I just like to keep an eye on everything going on here on the island." Levi tipped his hat toward the man. "Have a great day."

Levi had just met the man, and he already didn't like him. Something more than met the eye was going on with that land.

Levi needed to figure out exactly what that was.

"YOU LOOK TENSE," Dani said as Levi climbed back into the Jeep. His shoulders seemed tight, his eyes narrow, and his steps more brisk than usual.

He threw the vehicle into Drive. "It's that obvious?"

"I suppose it is. I take it those people aren't your favorite." She nodded toward the men in the distance.

"Just met them today."

"And so many hard feelings already?" Maybe Dani should stop asking the questions. But the whole situation was curious.

"Those men are trying to buy that land."

"And that's a problem?" She couldn't figure out island dynamics. Other people had built homes here. What was wrong with these people doing the same?

"Problem? Maybe that's an overstatement. But we're fighting too much development here on the island. Those horses need places to roam free. If some people have their way, this will become another resort community."

She nodded, Levi's perspective making more sense. "I see. There's nothing you can do to stop them, I take it?"

"We're doing everything within our power. Unfortunately, it seems like money always wins. This is the second stretch of property this has happened on. Another lot closer to town has also been bought up. My only comfort is in knowing these people need an easement to get to their property. But now that Mr. Wilkes has passed..."

"Who is Mr. Wilkes?"

"He was a bit of a loner around here. He lived in an old house not far from Wash Woods. He didn't let people get too close, but he loved this island."

"He doesn't have any other family?"

"He came from a large family. The Wilkes name pops up all over the tombstones in town. Anyway, Ed passed away a few weeks ago. About four months ago, he went to live in a nursing home up in Virginia. I guess that's why it took so long to hear about his death."

"So the land will go to his next of kin?"

"We can only assume."

"And who is that?" Dani asked.

Levi shrugged. "Your guess is as good as mine. I didn't think he had any kids, so maybe a nephew or niece?"

Dani glanced at the area around her again. "It does seem like it would be a shame to have the beauty around us destroyed."

"If people let it, Cape Corral would become another Nags Head. Do you know where that is?"

"That's the resort town farther south from here, correct?"

Levi nodded. "Correct. I don't suppose you remember ever going there?"

"Not really. But it seems familiar at the same time." Dani shook her head, wishing answers would come more easily than they were.

"Maybe something will ring a bell eventually."

She could only hope.

But Levi still seemed preoccupied with his earlier confrontation.

"Maybe Mr. Wilkes's next of kin won't sell the land for that easement after all," Dani finally said, trying to find some encouraging words. "If the locals are as adamant as you say they are about defending this island, then why would they?"

"Like I said, too often it goes back to money, even when it comes to the people that we least expect. Plus, we don't even know who his next of kin is."

"I am sorry to hear that. I hope everything works out for you."

Just then, someone flagged them down. Levi pulled to the side of the road and waited as an older gentleman walked toward his window. "This is Mr. Henderson. He's one of our volunteer Sanctuary Watchers, and he was a police officer in a small town not far from here until he retired about twenty years ago."

"Just thought I'd let you know that there's been some strange activity going on down by the Currituck Sound," the man started, leaning into the window of the Jeep. "Lots of boats coming and going."

"You'd know since you live right on the water," Levi said.

"I'm trying to track down the person who's dropping people off in the middle of the night. Not that there's anything illegal about it—but it is suspicious. So far, I've had no luck."

"Keep working on that, would you?" Levi said. "I'll put in a few requests myself. Maybe I need to start having the Coast Guard monitor the Currituck a little bit more to make sure nothing illegal is going on."

Dani's mind raced. Deserted waters seemed like the perfect place for bad things to happen. Things like drugs or other kinds of smuggling.

The more she learned about Levi, the more she realized that he really did have a big job—a job she didn't envy.

CHAPTER THIRTY-EIGHT

AS LEVI'S PHONE RANG, he glanced at the screen and frowned.

It was Langston, calling about that job offer up in Maine. Levi wasn't ready to talk to him about it. He hit Silence and put the phone back in his pocket.

"Everything okay?" Dani asked.

Levi glanced at her, and guilt pressed on him. When she'd asked him earlier if he could see himself staying here for a long time, he hadn't been truthful with her. Yet, he hadn't told anybody about that job offer. He didn't want to get people upset for no reason, especially if he decided to stay in Cape Corral.

"Look, I wasn't entirely honest with you earlier. The truth is, I've been offered a job up in Maine as a police chief."

Dani's eyes widened. "Wow. That seems like that would be a big change."

He nodded grimly. "It would be. But I can't help but wonder if it would be for the best."

"And why do you think that? I thought you had everything that you wanted here."

The way she said the words made Levi remember what he would be giving up. "I do have so much here. But the fact of the matter is that wherever I go and wherever I look brings memories of Adrienne."

"She was your wife?"

Levi nodded stiffly. "That's right. She's been gone for three years."

"I can't imagine how difficult that must be. I'm sorry."

"In some ways, it's gotten easier. I don't wake up in the morning expecting her to still be beside me. New routines have set in, and I moved into a new house—a house without any of her touches. I was hoping that might be easier."

"If you don't mind me asking, what happened?"

Levi rubbed his jaw for a moment and stared out the window. "Adrienne loved horseback riding. In fact, she began to do some things competitively. But her horse got spooked by a snake. He reared up and threw her off. When that happened, her head hit a tree. Her death was instantaneous."

"I'm so sorry." Dani reached forward and

squeezed his forearm before quickly drawing her hand back to herself.

"I wrestled with what happened for a long time. The truth is, I'll never make sense of it. I'll never understand why someone so good and pure died while other people who are so violent and dark are alive and thriving."

"I'm sure that's a question a lot of people have to ask themselves after tragedy. And there's no good answer. At least, there's not a good answer this side of heaven."

Levi nodded, appreciating the understanding in her voice.

As he glanced over at her, his breath caught.

What was it about Dani that made him feel like maybe he could move on? That possibility was dangerous. He still didn't know enough about her to make any decision like that.

When the sun hit her face and her eyes glimmered with kindness, he felt hope. Maybe he could move on. Maybe his future wasn't meant to be spent all alone as he had thought.

DANI AND LEVI continued to patrol the island. She couldn't help but feel like they'd somehow bonded. Which was strange. She shouldn't be bonding with anyone. She didn't even know who she was.

Yet it had happened. Somehow, she felt closer to Levi than she had before. She was honored that he'd opened up to her.

"Can you show me the dock where I came to the island?" Dani asked.

Levi glanced at her, not bothering to hide his surprise. "If you think it would help, sure."

She braced herself, hating the tension building in her. She really didn't want to find out that she was on the wrong side of the law. But she needed answers.

A few minutes later, Levi pulled to a stop in front of a boat ramp. On either side of it were docks that the public could use. Just across the water, she could see a strip of land, commonly referred to around here as the "mainland." That's what Levi had told her earlier, at least.

She climbed out and stood on the weathered wooden planks. As the breeze blew over her, she pulled her arms around herself.

She was keenly aware of Levi standing behind her. He wasn't too close—but he was close enough that she could feel his presence.

"This really is beautiful," she murmured.

"It is."

"It seems like such a shame for you to leave this

behind." Dani turned toward him, wanting to see his eyes.

As she did, their gazes caught.

There was something there. Something between them. She could sense it.

Both of them stared at the other as if unable to break the moment.

Dani licked her lips, wondering what it would be like if Levi kissed her. Wondered what it would feel like to have his strong arms around her.

It was a bad idea. She knew it was.

But that didn't lessen her desire.

"Dani." Levi stepped closer.

She didn't put any space between them. "Yes?"

He opened his mouth, about to say something as his gaze flickered down to her lips.

But before any words emerged, a sound pulled them from the moment.

The rustling came from the brush in the distance.

Had trouble found them?

CHAPTER THIRTY-NINE

LEVI STEPPED BACK, his muscles instantly tightening.

"Stay here." His voice left no room for questions.

He strode across the sandy banks toward the thick vegetation in the distance. If someone was trying to hide there, they were doing a poor job of it. What was going on?

He glanced behind him and saw Dani standing there. One arm was in a sling and her other was flung across her chest atop the sling as she stared after him.

Levi's heart pounded with concern. He didn't want anything to happen to her.

He had failed Adrienne, but he was determined not to fail Dani also.

His hand went to the gun in his holster, and he pulled it out.

"Hello?" he called. "This is the police. Come out with your hands up."

He waited, but nothing happened. The rustling continued.

Levi continued to creep closer, still on guard and still expecting the worst.

The sound seemed to move farther away.

Was the person who was hiding in these woods running away?

Levi couldn't let that happen. Yet he didn't want to leave Dani either.

He glanced back at her, knowing that he had to make a decision.

And he had to make it quickly.

DANI CROUCHED as low as she could, wanting to disappear. But there was nowhere to go. There was only a dock beneath her and open water behind her. If the person in the brush had a gun, she would be a goner.

Her heart thumped in her ears with trepidation.

As Levi strode toward the sound, she lifted up a prayer. *Please, be with him. Please. I can't handle anything happening to him, especially if it's my fault.*

Who was out there in those woods? And what was going to happen next?

All she could do was watch and wait.

Could it be possible that she had already started to care about Levi in the short time they'd known each other? It seemed too quick. She'd be lying if she didn't admit that there was some type of connection between them that she wanted to explore.

It was better that they hadn't kissed. She didn't know enough about her past to take that step. Giving in to the moment wouldn't have been a wise idea.

But her lips still burned at the thought of it.

She saw some tree branches moving, and she braced herself for whatever was about to happen.

Levi stood on the shore, glancing back at her before gazing at the movement again. He braced himself with a gun in his hand. She could tell that he was trying to figure out whether or not to step into the brush or to stay close to her.

The decision seemed to be made for him.

The next instant, a horse darted from the woods.

A foal.

Was that Skeeter? Dani didn't know enough about the horse to say for sure.

She let out the breath she'd held.

At least it wasn't a gunman.

CHAPTER FORTY

DANI WATCHED as a small group of the saltwater cowboys gathered around Skeeter. The horse had been taken to a stable area to be checked out. Acadia had come out to examine the horse.

As all that happened, Dani stood near the fence and watched the events unfolding. It was unlike anything she'd ever experienced before.

Who would have ever thought she would have ended up on an island full of cowboys and wild horses? If circumstances were different, she might actually even enjoy this.

Finally, Levi strode back toward her, adjusting his hat as he approached.

"How is he?" Dani asked.

"A little dehydrated, but Acadia thinks he'll be fine."

That was a relief, at least. "Do you know what happened?"

"Some kind of leash was put around his neck and my guess is that he was tied to something, maybe a tree."

Dani sucked in a breath. "Why would someone do that?"

"I have a theory, but it's only that. A theory."

"What are you thinking?" Dani felt the tension thread between her shoulders as she waited for his answer.

"I have a feeling that someone tied Skeeter up to distract us."

"To distract you from what?"

"Whatever is going on here on the island. They knew that we'd be looking for the horse and that would take up our time. It was almost a sleight of hand trick."

"That's terrible."

"I think Paul Robinson was probably involved in taking this horse. And I'm guessing that Skeeter's mom kicked the man while trying to protect her foal and that's how Paul ended up dying."

Dani shook her head. "I'll never understand people."

"Horses seem to be much easier to understand sometimes, don't they?"

She felt her lip tugging up at the start of a grin.

"Maybe for you. I don't think I know that much about horses. But I would like to learn."

Now why had she said that? Was she implying that she might want to stay here in Cape Corral? That thought was crazy. Somewhere out there she had another life waiting for her.

Levi's gaze seemed to burn into her. Dani felt his eyes watching her, and she reached out to touch the tips of her hair.

After a second, he looked away, and the moment was broken. "Let me get you back. You don't need to push yourself too hard. Your body is still healing."

She nodded. She had to admit that she was a little tired. Even though the day wasn't too hot, when the sun hit her unobstructed it did seem to make all of her energy evaporate like dew on the grass blades in the morning.

"That sounds good. If Skeeter will be okay, of course."

Levi nodded as he stepped toward the gate. "Grant is going to stay here, as well as Acadia. Skeeter is in good hands, but I'll come back later to check on him again."

With that, Levi placed his hand on the small of her back and guided her back to the Jeep.

LEVI PAUSED in the living room of the inn and turned to face Dani. He didn't know what was going on between them. But he did know he'd come close to kissing her earlier.

He knew he had no business kissing her right now. For so many reasons.

Despite all his logic, his heart couldn't deny there was something special about Dani. Yet, there were still too many obstacles between them to pursue anything. The fact that Levi had been interrupted before he could kiss her was a blessing in disguise. But he couldn't deny his attraction to the woman.

She's going to leave this island one day, he silently told himself. *And you still don't know how she's connected with these crimes.*

There were so many reasons to stay away.

But as he stared at Dani now, nearly all of those reasons disappeared from his mind.

"Thanks for coming with me today," he said.

"Thanks for letting me tag along. I'm glad that Skeeter was found. At least that's one less thing on your list to worry about."

"At least." Levi opened his mouth, not sure what else was going to come out. But he felt like there was so much that he could say to her right now.

Nighttime was starting to fall. It had been a

long day. And he needed to get back to the stables to check on Skeeter.

"Look, Dani. About earlier—"

"You don't have to say anything," she said.

So she'd felt it too.

"But I feel like I do," he said.

Dani's wide eyes stared at him, questions floating there.

"I just wish that circumstances were different—"

Before Levi could finish the statement, a knock sounded at the door. He quickly shut his mouth and offered an apologetic look. "I should get that."

She nodded. "You probably should."

Hesitantly, Levi stepped away. He pulled the door open, unsure whom he was expecting to see.

A stranger stood there.

"Hi, my name is Aaron Demoss. I'm here looking for my girlfriend." He held up a picture. "I was hoping that you may have seen her."

Levi sucked in a breath as he studied the photo on the man's phone.

It was Dani.

CHAPTER FORTY-ONE

DANI SAW the photo on the man's phone and gasped.

It was a picture of her.

Except in the photo, her dark hair was long and flowy. Her outfit was pristine. Her smile was bright, and her eyes confident.

The contrast between the woman in this image and the broken woman Dani now was couldn't have been more obvious.

Her gaze flashed back toward the man standing near the door. She waited for a memory to hit her.

But nothing came.

Levi glanced at her, his eyes narrow and protective.

As he did, the man spotted Dani. He stepped into the room, and his shoulders seemed to slump with relief.

"Dani. You're here. You're okay!" The next instant, he wrapped his arms around her in a loose hug, carefully avoiding her injury.

Guilt pressed at her. Dani thought she should return the gesture. But she couldn't do that. No matter how happy this man was to see her, she had no clue who he was. The name Aaron Demoss didn't ring any bells.

Levi moved closer to them. "Maybe you should give her a little space."

Aaron stepped back and looked at him, a wrinkle forming between his eyes. Then he turned back to Dani. "How did you get here? What happened?"

Dani opened her mouth to speak but shut it again. How much did she say? Was this man even the real deal? With everything that was going on, she needed to be certain.

Thankfully, Levi took charge. "Why don't you sit down? We need to talk."

The man had thick muscles and stood at least six foot four inches tall. As Levi addressed him, the man's gaze darkened and his hands went to his hips. He obviously didn't like the way things were going right now.

Despite that, he lowered himself onto the couch, though he made no effort to relax.

The knot between his eyes grew larger when Dani sat across from him instead of beside him.

"I'm going to need some more information from you," Levi started.

Aaron's gaze swung between Dani and Levi. "I don't know what's going on here. But I've been looking for Dani for the past four days. Now that I've found her, I feel like I'm being interrogated. Dani, I can't tell you how glad I am that you're okay. You've had a lot of people worried about you."

People had been worried about her? The words were like music to Dani's ears. For the entire time she'd been on the island, Dani had assumed she had no one. And if she had no one, that meant she'd been unlovable and unlikable.

So many questions collided in her mind, and Dani didn't know what to do with any of them. She was so grateful that Levi could help her wade through these unfamiliar waters. Right now, she could hardly breathe, nonetheless think clearly.

"When was the last time you saw Dani?" Levi said.

"Monday evening." Aaron studied her. "You don't remember any of this?"

She rubbed her free hand on her jeans. "No, I'm sorry. I don't."

The man shook his head ever so slightly. "I don't understand."

Dani glanced at Levi who gave her a subtle nod. "I've lost most of my memories."

Aaron sucked in a breath before hanging his

head. "Then it's true. Everything is suddenly making sense."

LEVI'S MUSCLES bristled with caution. He would remain this way until he knew that this man was legit.

"Would you mind telling us what happened the last time you saw Dani?" Levi started.

More than anything, he wanted to sit next to her. To place his hand on her back to offer her some comfort. To assure her he'd always be there to protect her.

But if this man really was Dani's boyfriend, the best thing Levi could do was to maintain his distance. Until he knew for sure, he would do everything within his power to protect her.

Aaron frowned. "Maybe it's a blessing that you can't remember when we were together last."

"What do you mean?" Dani's voice cracked as she asked the question. She looked as if her future hung in the balance. Like she couldn't breathe. Like her head was spinning. Even her skin . . . it looked so pale.

"You and I were going out on a trip to see my mom and dad," Aaron started. "We pulled into a rest station near the Virginia/North Carolina border. As soon as I unlocked the doors so we could get out, two men jumped in the back seat."

Levi listened carefully, trying to reserve his judgment until he heard the whole story.

"One of the men had a gun. He forced me to drive down some back roads in North Carolina. I had no choice but to do what he said. I was afraid . . . I was afraid he was going to shoot you." Aaron seemed to choke the words out.

"And then what?" Levi's voice sounded harder than he intended. But he couldn't let down his guard yet.

"We pulled up to a harbor by the water. It was getting dark, and Dani and I were both shaking like leaves in an earthquake. These men blindfolded us and put us on a boat. I begged them to let us go. But they said they had other plans for us."

"Did you catch a glimpse of these men's faces?" Levi asked.

Aaron shook his head before running a hand over his face. "No, I didn't. Like I said, they were in the back seat, and then we were blindfolded."

Levi crossed his arms. "What happened next?"

"We got off the boat on a beach. I didn't know where we were. It was getting dark outside, and they led us through some brush. Said that we needed to give them everything in our bank accounts. If we didn't, they were going to kill us. I figured that they were going to kill us either way, but I didn't know what to do." His gaze traveled to Dani and he frowned. "Dani was a mess. She was quivering, and I was terrified of what might happen."

"Was this one of the men?" Levi held up his phone, showing a picture of Paul Robertson.

Aaron tilted his head in uncertainty. "I can't say for sure. Like I said it was dark. That man looks vaguely familiar."

Levi lowered his phone. "Did you give them your money?"

"We did an electronic transfer. Told these guys we'd do whatever it took just to get them to let us go."

"Do you think that they targeted you from the start?"

"I can only assume that." Aaron drew in a deep breath, his face twisting as if he tried to hold back his emotions. Finally, he wiped his hand across his features and sucked in another deep breath. "I'm not sure why they had to take us to the island to do all of this instead of just doing it in the car. It wasn't like I could ask any questions."

Levi had asked himself that same question. What purpose would that serve? There had to be more to this story.

"Keep going," Levi continued.

"As soon as Dani and I gave this man our money, I saw an opportunity to run." Aaron's voice caught. "I grabbed Dani's hand, and we took off. We made it back to the boat, and I thought we were home free. But the motor stalled. The man . . . he pulled the trigger. The bullet hit Dani."

"Was she shot from the front or the back?" Levi put the question out there as a test.

Aaron flinched, as if the question triggered bad memories. "She looked back for a minute and that's when this guy shot her. It hit between her shoulder and heart. I stopped and knelt on the ground to help her. She was obviously in a lot of pain. But the man pulled me away and separated us."

"And then?"

Aaron shifted on the couch, moisture glimmering in his eyes. "He hit me over the head, and everything went black. When I woke up, I was on the side of the road up near Richmond. Dani was nowhere to be seen."

"Did you report what happened to the police?"

"I was going to. But I got a text saying Dani was alive and being held captive. He said if I spoke about anything, he'd finish Dani off. I didn't know if this guy was bluffing or not, but I couldn't take any chances."

"So how did you end up here?" Levi asked.

"I didn't know what else to do, so I started trying to find her myself. I tried to retrace our steps from the rest stop and my search led here. I began asking around. I ran into a nice lady at the house I'm renting. She said something about a suspicious woman with amnesia and an injury who was staying at the inn."

Mary Lou. She must have caught wind of Dani's story. It didn't take long for word to spread here. Plus, Mary Lou may have mentioned Dani to this man just out of spite or jealousy.

Levi's muscles bristled even more.

"I see." Levi supposed that the man's story seemed plausible, but he still wasn't 100 percent certain.

"When I heard amnesia . . . honestly, I still didn't know if it was you, Dani, or how much you might remember. I mean, sometimes people remember their names and only forget the trauma, right?"

"That's what I've heard," Dani mumbled.

"You've forgotten everything?" He stared at her, his bottom lip parting in what looked like shock.

"That's correct."

He lowered his voice. "I'm sorry to hear that. But I can't believe you're here. You're okay."

"It's been quite the journey, to say the least," Dani said.

Aaron's gaze remained on Dani. "How did you end up here at this inn? What happened—that you remember? I can't get the image of you being shot out of my head. I hoped you might have survived but . . . I fully expected this guy to still be holding you hostage."

Dani glanced at her hands and shrugged, looking as confused as Levi might imagine her to be. "I washed up on the shore, and Levi found me. But the only thing I know is my first name."

Aaron stared at her. "Really? Nothing else?"

"No, nothing."

He started to reach for her but pulled his hand back and frowned. More moisture welled in his eyes as he gazed at her. "I'm so glad you're okay. I thought the guys were bluffing, that they'd already killed you. I had to know for myself."

Levi had a lot of facts to check out before he would trust this man. It didn't matter how many tears he cried. Levi was only sticking to the facts.

CHAPTER FORTY-TWO

QUESTIONS SWIRLED in Dani's head. There was still so much that she needed to know. But this man's story sounded plausible. In her situation, it was just so hard to know who to trust.

"What's my last name?" she finally asked.

"Your last name is Dodson," Aaron said.

"Dani Dodson?" She said the words aloud, hoping they would ring a bell.

They didn't.

"I put out a search for any missing persons named Dani, Danielle, or Daniela." Levi's voice still contained a hard edge. "I didn't get any hits."

"Like I said, I couldn't report her missing," Aaron said. "I didn't want to chance it. But there's another reason for that also. Her official first name is Idania. Apparently, it's a family name."

Idania? How unique.

"Where am I from?" Dani asked.

"You live outside Richmond in a town called Chesterfield. You work as a meeting planner. You do a great job. You're in high demand and travel quite a bit."

"None of my coworkers noticed I was missing?" Her throat tightened as she waited for his response.

"No one thought much of it because the two of us were supposed to be visiting my parents. You'd taken a week off work and asked everyone not to call you. Said you wanted to unplug. So no one is suspicious. Yet. I suspect that come Monday if you don't show back up for work, they will be."

Dani stared at Aaron's face, trying to imagine it was familiar. But nothing clicked in place. What if it never did?

She licked her lips, not liking the thought of that. "How long have you and I dated?"

"About three months. We met through some mutual friends. Our first date, we went ice skating. I fell and you laughed at me. That's when I knew we were supposed to be together." He flashed a sad smile.

Dani wanted to return the smile, to feel warm and fuzzy feelings. But none were there still.

"Do you have any pictures of the two of you together?" Levi's rigid voice cut into the moment.

"Pictures?" Aaron repeated before reaching into

his pocket and pulling out his phone. "Yes. Of course."

Dani held her breath as she waited to see what he found.

He swiped through several things on his screen before finally handing the phone to Levi. Levi brought the device over to Dani so she could also see. Gratitude filled her—she felt beside herself as she waited to see Aaron's "proof."

Sure enough, pictures of Dani and Aaron smiling beside each other stared back. One of the photos looked like they were at a party. Another one had the mountains behind them. Still another showed them at a restaurant.

And truthfully, they looked happy together.

Dani's head began to throb. It just didn't make any sense to her.

But this man seemed to have evidence of her real life. Why would he lie?

She didn't know. But Dani was going to have to figure out her next step.

If that next step included leaving Cape Corral, her heart might just break a little bit.

LEVI STILL WASN'T comfortable with this situation and he wasn't ready to turn Dani over to this stranger. Not until he did some digging.

"I'm going to need to verify everything you've told us." Levi's gaze burned into the man's.

Aaron's gaze flickered. "Of course. Do whatever you need to do. With this situation it isn't unexpected. This sure isn't the way I thought our trip would go."

Just then, the front door burst open, and Emmy and Colby rushed inside, their eyes lit with excitement.

"I heard Skeeter was found," Emmy rushed. But her words fell flat as her gaze fell on Aaron. "I'm sorry. I didn't realize we had a guest here."

"Emmy, Colby, this is Aaron Demoss. He came here looking for Dani."

The smile slipped from Emmy's face. "Wow. I mean, that's great. That's what we wanted, right?"

"Absolutely," Dani said, her words unconvincing.

Levi rose, knowing he needed to use this opportunity to do some research. "Listen, I need to make a few phone calls. Would you two mind sticking around and making our guest feel . . . at home?"

"Of course." Emmy glanced back at Aaron and attempted a smile. "No problem."

But Levi still felt hesitant to leave them. He had no other choice right now.

He pulled Aaron aside to get some additional information and to look at his driver's license.

Aaron gave him the name of some mutual friends who should be able to verify his story.

Levi gave one last glance at Dani as he stepped toward Emmy's bedroom to follow up on the situation. He could use his sister's computer and still stay close.

He wouldn't have any peace until he confirmed the details Aaron had shared.

The first place he called was the company Dani supposedly worked for. Her boss confirmed that Dani was employed there and had taken some days off. She'd said Dani was private, but she had mentioned someone named Aaron in the past.

He also called one of Dani's friends, someone Aaron had mentioned. The woman, someone named Carolyn Thomas, answered on the first ring. Levi explained to her who he was.

"I understand that you and Dani are friends," he started.

"That's right. We work together. Is she okay?"

Levi really didn't think Dani was fine at all, not given everything that had happened. But he didn't need to tell this woman that. "She's . . . fine. Listen, we're following up on a lead with one of our investigations. Can you tell me if Dani is dating anyone?"

The woman paused. "What's this about? Everything doesn't sound okay. Police don't usually call and ask about someone's dating life."

"There was an accident. Dani is fine. I just need to verify some details."

Carolyn gasped. "An accident?"

"Like I said, Dani is fine. I assure you."

"I'm glad to hear that." Carolyn paused. "She met some guy named Aaron not too long ago. They've been seeing each other on a casual basis."

"Can you tell me what he looks like?"

"Sure. He's probably six foot four, and he has broad shoulders and dark hair. He seemed nice enough, and Dani seemed over the moon about him."

An unseen weight pressed on Levi. "If I send you a picture from my phone can you verify that it's him?"

"Of course. I'm sorry to hear that there was an accident. Is there anything I can do?"

Levi frowned. "Not now. But if anything comes up, I'll give you a call."

"Do that. And tell Dani that I'm praying for her. I can't imagine what she's going through right now."

It looked like Aaron's story was the truth.

Why did that fact fill Levi with utter disappointment?

CHAPTER FORTY-THREE

EMMY AND COLBY sat on a bench near the stairway and attempted some small talk. But Dani hardly heard any of it. She just stared at Aaron, trying to imagine the two of them together. She hadn't pictured someone like Aaron as being her type.

Which was silly.

What type had she envisioned herself with?

Her throat tightened. She knew.

Someone like Levi.

She'd have to think about that later.

"What about my parents?" Dani remembered that vision she'd had of her sixteenth birthday, and the man and the woman holding the cake, smiling down at her.

Aaron frowned. "I'm sorry to tell you this, Dani, but they died three years ago in an accident. They were RVing across the United States when a storm came up and a tree hit their vehicle."

Her heart pounded with grief that she couldn't fully understand. But his words made sense. In her gut, she had known that her parents weren't alive anymore.

"Do I live by myself?"

"You do. You have a condo. You like to be around people, but you also like time to yourself." Aaron shifted. "I know this is hard for you. I can't imagine what you might be thinking right now."

Dani nodded, not knowing what else to say. This man felt like such a stranger. Yet they'd been dating.

"Just know that you have a safe place when you get back home, and people will take care of you," Aaron continued, his eyes imploring her. "You don't need to stay here with strangers in a strange place. Besides, once you see your condo, maybe things will start clicking in place."

His words made sense. Even though Dani didn't want to believe him, she had no reason not to. He had pictures of the two of them together. He seemed nice enough. Certainly, Levi would look into his background and confirm he was safe.

So why did Dani feel unsettled?

"These men who were after us . . . don't you think they'll track us down if I leave here with you?" Her throat burned as the question left her lips.

"Now that I know you're safe, we can go to the police," Aaron said. "Law enforcement here already knows, but we should report it to the police in Chesterfield also. In the meantime, Carolyn said we could stay with her. She has a place in the mountains where we can lie low until this blows over."

Just then, Levi stepped out of Emmy's bedroom where he'd been making phone calls for the past thirty minutes. By the stiff way he nodded, Dani knew she needed to brace herself for whatever he had to say.

"I talked to one of your friends, and she verified that you and Aaron were dating." Levi's voice sounded tense.

Dani glanced at Aaron again, the concept of being with him feeling so foreign.

"Your friend also confirmed that you were an event planner and that you lived by yourself in Chesterfield, Virginia," Levi continued. "Your parents died in an auto accident several years ago. I was also able to check your bank account and verify that a large sum of money was transferred from it on Monday evening."

Dani supposed that should be good news. But all she could do was sit there, feeling like her whole world had been rocked.

"I also looked into your background, Aaron." Levi turned to the man on the couch. "You're a lawyer. No record. Nothing that raises any warning flags."

"I appreciate your diligence, but what's our next step?" Aaron asked. "It's getting dark, and I don't want to leave the island too late. But I'm anxious to get Dani back."

"I'll need to clear her with the doctor before she can leave. The earliest I can see that happening is in the morning."

"You're welcome to stay here in the meantime," Emmy offered. "Besides, how did you plan on leaving? The bridge is washed out."

"I found someone across the water who brought me over in his boat," Aaron said. "He gave me his number. Said to call when I needed a ride back. If staying here tonight is what I need to do, then that's what I'll do. I'll take one of your rooms."

"I can show you where you'll be staying." Emmy nodded toward the staircase.

With one last glance at Dani, Aaron followed after Emmy.

As soon as he was gone, Dani released the breath she held. Finally, her lungs loosened.

Why did she feel apprehensive?

Anyone in her situation would, right?

But there was another part of her that wanted to turn back time.

LEVI LISTENED as Dani and Aaron caught up with each other. He couldn't bring himself to leave them alone.

Something about the whole situation made his apprehension rise.

He could tell that Dani was trying to be polite. She listened and nodded and asked questions. But she also remained standoffish—as she should. Levi hadn't talked to Dr. Knightly, but it seemed unwise to act as if she trusted a virtual stranger.

"Levi, could you help me with some of these dishes?" Emmy asked.

Hesitantly, Levi rose from the table and walked over to the sink with her.

"Why are you giving our guest a death glare?" Emmy whispered.

"I don't know what you're talking about." Levi plucked a dish from the soapy water and began to scrub it.

"If your eyes could burn holes into someone, that's exactly what they would be doing now."

Levi didn't know what to say about that, so he remained quiet.

"You really think this guy is the real thing?" Emmy continued.

"He checks out."

"But you still have reservations."

"The situation is tricky. It would be for anyone."

"I can't deny that. I was just getting used to having her around here. Doesn't seem right that she's going to leave."

He stole a glance at Dani over his shoulder. Aaron said something and Dani let out a little laugh.

A stab of jealousy pricked him, and he ground his teeth together again before saying, "I agree."

Finally, thirty minutes of small talk later, Aaron excused himself to go up to bed. As soon as he did, Levi asked Dani if they could talk on the back porch for a minute.

"Of course." She rose and stepped with him out into the humid air, almost looking relieved.

They sat on the glider rockers and silence stretched for a few minutes. Levi's thoughts raced. How much should he say? Should he beg her to stay? He knew he couldn't do that. It wouldn't be fair to Dani. But he didn't want her to leave either.

"How are you feeling about this?" Levi honestly wanted to know.

"I'm feeling overwhelmed, to be honest." She glanced down at her hand in her lap. "I can't imagine leaving here tomorrow with that guy."

"That guy is your boyfriend."

She sighed. "He doesn't *feel* like my boyfriend. And leaving here doesn't feel like going home. It feels like *leaving* home."

Something about Dani's words warmed Levi's heart.

"You could always stay," Levi offered.

She cut a sharp glance his way. "But could I? How responsible would that be? And where would I live? How would I support myself?"

"You could stay at Emmy's and help her with the inn. Get a job with Mrs. Minnie at the Screen Porch Café. Help with a rental management company."

She let out a soft chuckle. "That's tempting. It really is."

Their gazes caught. Levi wanted to tell her how he felt.

But it was too late for that now. Levi wouldn't be that guy who tried to steal someone else's girlfriend.

But how was he going to let her go?

CHAPTER FORTY-FOUR

DANI HAD HARDLY BEEN able to sleep all night. All she could think about was leaving.

She didn't have any possessions to take with her other than the "Dani" necklace adorning her neck. She would leave the clothes Emmy had let her borrow here. It only made sense.

But all Dani could think about was the fact that she wanted to stay. But she couldn't in good conscience do that. It would be . . . irresponsible.

Dread pooled in her stomach as she showered and got ready for the day. When she got back to her place, she'd mail Emmy some money for the clothes she was wearing home as well as for her room and board.

Home?

It seemed like such a foreign word.

Not a place several hours away from here.

With no other choice, Dani trudged downstairs and spotted Aaron at the breakfast table with Emmy. The two chatted amicably.

Her heart sank when she saw Levi wasn't here.

Dani had to get that man out of her system—especially if she was dating someone else.

But Aaron was a stranger to her. At least, he would remain that way until Dani started remembering things. Sometimes, it felt like it would be forever before that happened.

"Good morning." Aaron's eyes lit when he saw her, and he stood.

Dani felt almost shy as she nodded back to him and murmured, "Morning."

She sat across from him at the table. As she did, Emmy set a slice of breakfast casserole in front of her. "Eat up. You're going to have a long day today."

Dani raised her fork, but she had no desire to eat. The thought of food being in her stomach made her feel nauseated.

"Good news," Aaron said. "Emmy was telling me that the doctor is going to stop by in just thirty minutes. After he checks you, we should be cleared to go."

"You're right, that is good news." But as Dani said her final two words, her voice broke.

"It's okay to be nervous," Aaron murmured. "Anybody in your shoes would be."

Relief washed through Dani. At least he understood that.

But Dani continued to pick at her food. How was she going to get through this day?

She wasn't sure.

Because a part of her just wanted to run and forget that Aaron had ever shown up.

LEVI GLANCED AT HIS WATCH. He still had fifteen minutes until Dr. Knightly was supposed to visit Dani.

He'd stayed up for most of the night, working and trying to find out anything else he could about this Aaron Demoss guy. If there was anything shady going on, Levi needed to figure out what before Dani left with this guy.

Otherwise, Levi couldn't keep her here for no reason. But if he could find something that proved things weren't on the up and up, then maybe Dani would stay.

He looked up from his computer and ran a hand over his face. Had he lost his mind? Levi had known better than to get personally involved with someone he was working with. Yet he had, and now he was in deep.

Best he could tell, Aaron Demoss checked out. Dani really did work for an event planning organization. Her parents really were dead. And she really did have a lease on a place in Chesterfield, Virginia.

Everything had been checked off. So why did Levi still feel so hesitant?

He knew why.

Because he didn't want to let Dani go.

Someone knocked at the door just then. Acadia stepped in.

"Morning, Levi. I just wanted to give you the update that Skeeter is doing fine."

"That's good to hear. Is our original theory correct? Was he tethered to a tree out in the middle of Wash Woods?"

She frowned as she nodded. "That's how it appears. I can't believe somebody would do that to him. The good news is, he wasn't harmed in the process. It could have turned out a lot different."

"That is good news. Thanks for taking care of that."

"No problem." She started to take a step back when she paused. "I hear our mystery lady here on the island finally has a name."

"That's right."

"That's good news, right?"

"We still don't know all that happened to her. But I can't force her to stay here either."

Acadia studied him for a minute. "You're suspicious still, aren't you?"

Levi didn't deny it. "There are just too many unanswered questions for me to be comfortable."

"I agree. Something bad happened on this island, and our mystery woman is connected with it."

Levi had been through the story that Aaron told him more than once.

There was one thing that didn't make sense to him.

Aaron had said he'd been forced to this island by coercion. But those two campers that Levi had talked to—Barry and Gilbert—had said that the three people they saw walking through the island acted like they were good friends. There were no signs that anybody was forced to be here.

That fact bothered Levi. However, it had been getting dark outside. No doubt it had been hard to see.

Still, maybe Levi should go through Aaron's story with him one more time before he and Dani left the island. He needed to get an official statement anyway.

He glanced at his watch. It was time for Dr. Knightly to arrive. Levi had just enough time to get over there.

CHAPTER FORTY-FIVE

"YOU'RE GOOD TO GO." Dr. Knightly lowered his stethoscope back around his neck. "You'll just need to monitor that incision, and, if it turns red, you'll need to visit your general practitioner back in Virginia. Otherwise, you should be able to take that sling off in the next week or two."

The two of them sat in the living room at the inn. She could have asked for somewhere more private or asked for Aaron, Emmy, and Colby to step away. But there was no need for it. The doctor was simply looking at her wound and monitoring her vitals.

"Great," Dani finally choked out. She'd been secretly hoping he'd give her a reason to stay, but that hadn't happened.

"Your girlfriend really is very lucky." Dr. Knightly turned to Aaron. "If that bullet had been just a half an inch in any direction, she probably wouldn't be here right now."

Aaron placed his hand on Dani's back. "Believe me, I know how lucky I am."

He must have sensed Dani's muscles tense because he quickly pulled his arm down.

Dani definitely wasn't ready for him to touch her, even in a simple way as he'd just done.

"I guess this means we can go." Aaron looked at her, a tight smile on his face. "I'll put in the call to the charter boat so it can meet us at the docks. We'll just need to figure out how to get a ride there."

"Great." But the word didn't sound convincing as it left Dani's lips.

She couldn't possibly leave here without saying goodbye to Levi. It just seemed like such a shame. It seemed like more than a shame. The thought of it made panic want to rise inside her.

Dani turned toward Emmy, who waited in the background. "Thank you so much for everything. You've been a real lifesaver over the past several days."

Emmy pulled her into a long hug. "I'm so glad we got to know each other. It was fun having another girl around here for a little while."

"It was fun." Dani stepped back and looked at Colby. She wasn't sure whether to shake his hand or to hug him. But before she could decide, his arms wrapped around her shoulders.

"You take care of yourself, Dani," he said. "I think you're a natural around here, so you'll have to come back and visit."

Dani nodded. "I'd like that."

She glanced around one more time, realizing that Levi wasn't coming. Her gaze caught Emmy's, and the woman seemed to read Dani's disappointment.

"I'll tell Levi that you said goodbye," she murmured.

"Please do that. And thank him for everything that he did for me."

"Of course. I'd be happy to do that."

"I'll give you guys a ride to the boat docks." Colby pulled his keys out and swung them around his finger.

With one last wave at everyone, Dani stepped outside with Aaron and walked toward Colby's truck.

She couldn't help but feel like she was leaving part of her heart behind.

LEVI PULLED up to the inn just as Dani stepped outside with Aaron.

He put down his window and waved at them.

As Dani's eyes connected with his, Levi saw her gaze widen. She was just as happy to see him as he was to see her.

He didn't want her to leave. He'd thought about just letting her go, forgetting she was ever here.

But he couldn't do that. In the brief time they'd known each other, she'd somehow found a place in his heart.

"I'm glad I didn't miss you," Levi started. "Why don't you guys let me give you a ride down to the boat?"

"Colby already said that he would—" Aaron started.

"Sure," Dani interrupted. "That's a great idea."

Before Aaron could argue, Dani opened the door to Levi's truck and climbed inside. She scooted to the middle in order for Aaron to fit beside her. As she did, the scent of her strawberry-scented hair wafted around him.

He'd miss the aroma.

It wasn't too late, Levi told himself. Dani could still change her mind. Could still scrap this whole plan and just stay here.

But Levi knew Dani needed to return home. To figure out who she'd been. To check on her finances. To deal with her job and condo. She couldn't just leave someone else to handle all her problems. He just wished that things were different.

He cleared his throat as Aaron climbed in and slammed the door behind him. "I heard that Dr. Knightly cleared you."

"That's right." Dani's voice sounded surprisingly thin. "Apparently, my wound is healing up quite nicely."

"That's good." Levi nodded at the sky. "It's a good thing you're leaving now. That storm system is supposed to be here in two hours."

"It only takes about twenty minutes to get across the water, right?" Aaron peered around Dani as they bounced over the sand.

"That's right. As long as your captain is here on time, you should be okay. Who did you call, by the way? I know most of the captains who come out this way."

"A guy named RJ Hallowell," Aaron said. "You ever met him before?"

"Can't say I know his name." Levi knew most of the charter boat services around here. But that didn't mean that a new one hadn't popped up.

"He seemed to know the waters pretty well," Aaron continued. "Said he grew up down here on the Outer Banks."

"Makes sense. People who love the water tend to stay in this area. It's a waterman's paradise."

Levi hated all the chitchat. But what else was he supposed to talk about? Especially with Aaron here.

They reached the docks all too quickly, and they all climbed out. Sure enough, an older gentleman was waiting with a skiff. Levi waved at him before turning to Dani. His heart seemed to lodge in his throat as he did.

"Let me know how you're doing . . . if you don't mind," Levi started. "We've come this far together. I, at least, want to know that things are going well in your new old life."

Dani nodded, but Levi saw the tension on her face. She didn't want to leave either. "Of course. I'll definitely keep in touch. I can't tell you how much I appreciate everything that you've done for me."

"I'm going to keep investigating what happened to you. I haven't given up. In fact, I'll probably have more questions, especially given the new information Aaron shared."

She touched the wound at her shoulder. "I want to know who did this to me, so thank you."

There was so much that Levi wanted to say. But it wouldn't be beneficial for any of it to leave his lips. Instead, he squeezed her arm. "You take care of yourself, Dani."

"You too."

With a nod at Aaron, he watched the two of them walk down toward the dock.

And Levi realized he'd gotten too attached too quickly. But it was too late to do anything about it.

CHAPTER FORTY-SIX

SHE COULD DO THIS.

Dani would return home, get her affairs in order, and then she'd make a decision about her future. Just because she had fallen in love with this area didn't mean she was supposed to be here forever.

But Cape Corral would always hold a special place in her heart. She felt like she'd somehow found herself while in the middle of a crisis.

The wind whipped around her as she sat on the boat. With one last glance behind her, Dani saw the small island with its wild horses disappearing from sight. One of those legendary wild horses stood on the bank, almost as if he or she was sending Dani off.

Levi also stood there, still lingering near his truck as he watched the boat leave.

Her heart panged with a moment of agony. It seemed surreal that she'd be leaving him.

"It sounds like you really liked it there," Aaron said beside her, his arm casually draped across the back of the seat.

Dani felt a slight feeling of annoyance that he had interrupted her moment, but she tried to push it aside. There was no need to take this out on Aaron. He'd come all this way looking for her.

"There's something special about Cape Corral," Dani said.

"Maybe we can come back here one day then."

Coming back here with Aaron had no appeal, but Dani didn't tell him that. Once her memories came back, she might change her mind.

"Maybe," she said, knowing how noncommittal she sounded. "Is this your first time coming here?"

Something passed through Aaron's gaze as he nodded. "Well, second time officially if you count Monday as the first."

Dani supposed that would explain the look in his eyes. The situation must have been horrific. Maybe she should be glad she couldn't remember.

She cleared her throat, trying to turn her mind to more pleasant subjects. "The wild horses are absolutely fascinating."

"Who would have ever thought we had cowboys on the beach in North Carolina?"

"They do an important job."

Aaron glanced at her. "It sounds like you learned a lot about them in your short stay here."

She shrugged. "I guess I did."

As a few moments of silence fell, Dani pointed to the land on the other side of the Currituck Sound. "Aren't we supposed to be going that way?"

It seemed as if the boat had turned off course.

"The harbor area where I left my car isn't directly on the other side of the boat dock. It's a little more to the north."

Dani pushed down the bad feeling that brewed inside her, dismissing it as stress. The feeling was an accumulation of everything that had happened to her.

She hoped she didn't regret this. But she already did.

AS THE BOAT disappeared from sight, Levi walked back to his truck. He felt like part of him had just been lost. It didn't make sense. Then again, love rarely did.

Love? It was too early to be in love with Dani. But if she'd stayed around, Levi felt certain it could have led to that.

Just as he pulled his seatbelt across his chest, his phone rang.

It was Grant. Levi almost dismissed the call but

decided not to. Talking to his friend might be a good distraction.

"I know this might sound strange but there's something I think you need to know," Grant started.

Levi's muscles stiffened. "What's that?"

"Dani's real name . . . it sounded kind of familiar to me. I was talking to my neighbor when I happened to look over at the tombstone in his yard. The name there read Idania Wilkes."

Levi froze. He thought he knew what his friend was getting at, but he didn't want to jump to any conclusions. "You mean Mr. Wilkes had a relative also named Idania?"

"That's right. I started doing a little bit of research. I was curious about who Mr. Wilkes's land would go to now that he's deceased. We didn't know of any relatives but assumed that maybe he had a niece or nephew."

"Okay . . ."

"I talked to one of Mr. Wilkes's old neighbors, and it turns out that Mr. Wilkes was briefly married. He had a daughter who married someone with the last name of Dodson."

Levi sucked in a breath. "So what you're telling me is that Dani is the closest living relative of Mr. Wilkes?"

"That's right. And, based on everything I know,

as his granddaughter she would be next in line to get that land he left behind."

"So if somebody else who wanted that land got their hands on Dani . . ." He didn't want to finish the sentence.

"They might be able to convince her to sell the property to them. And if that didn't work . . ."

Levi knew what his friend was getting at. If that didn't work, they might kill her. Then the land would go up for public sale.

He stared in the direction the boat Dani was on had gone.

Levi needed to find a way to get to her.

There was no time to waste.

CHAPTER FORTY-SEVEN

DANI FELT sweat spreading across her skin.

Shouldn't they be at the dock by now? What was taking so long? Why was she so on edge?

She didn't have to answer that question. After everything she'd been through, it would be strange *not* to be on edge.

"Where exactly is this harbor?" Dani's hands gripped the seat beneath her as she asked the question.

"Not much longer," Aaron muttered, staring into the distance. "No worries. I've got everything taken care of."

Wouldn't it be nice to let someone else worry for her? But that wasn't an option. And Aaron wasn't who she'd choose to take that job either.

"How long a drive is it from the harbor to Chesterfield?" She needed to prepare herself for what was coming. The more she knew, the better off she would be.

Aaron offered a half shrug. "A few hours."

"I don't have a key to my apartment. Do you have one?" The questions continued to barrage her—the small details. Maybe focusing on the miniscule particulars made Dani feel some semblance of control. Or maybe she just talked a lot when she was nervous. She didn't know.

"I don't. But we'll figure out a way to get inside. Like I said, I'll take care of you."

Maybe she was worrying over nothing. But, even if that was the case, she couldn't seem to stop.

"I can't believe all of this is happening . . ." She stared out over the water and the whitecap waves that had started to form. Lightning flashed in the distance, promising that bad weather would soon be on them.

"I can't either," Aaron said. "I'm sorry, Dani."

As he said the words, a flashback swelled inside her.

I'm sorry, Dani.

Something about the words. About his voice.

It was familiar.

But why?

Dani rubbed her temples, trying to ignore the tension pulling across her forehead. She couldn't let this go. She had to remember.

She squeezed her eyes shut, praying the

memory would emerge. Whatever it was, it felt important. She could sense it.

Her mind jolted back in time.

She was on a boat.

It was stormy around her.

The sea raged.

And someone—a man—said, "I'm sorry, Dani."

Then the blast of gunfire pierced the air.

Fear hit her first—then the pain.

She gasped.

Not in her memory. But in real life. In present time.

She couldn't breathe as terror filled her.

"Dani?"

She jerked her eyes open. Aaron stared at her, his face suddenly seeming more familiar.

Had he been the one to pull the trigger?

Dani scooted backward in her seat as she tried to gather her thoughts—except there was nowhere to go.

She was trapped on this boat . . . with the man who'd shot her?

Aaron's face blurred in front of her. He wasn't a good man. In her gut, she knew that.

He'd been the one in her memory who'd apologized . . . right before he shot her.

As she stared at him now, something changed in his gaze.

He knew that she knew.

Dear Lord . . . what am I going to do?

LEVI SPOTTED a fisherman returning to a dock at a nearby house. He ran through the water—around the trees that filled the shoreline—until he reached the man.

He recognized him as Jason Henderson, a general contractor on the island.

Jason spotted Levi running toward him and froze.

"I need your boat," Levi muttered as he reached Jason.

"What?" Jason stared at him, looking baffled.

"I'll pay you for any gas or damages. But I need this boat. Now. Someone's life is on the line."

The man stared at him only another second before nodding. "Okay . . . I guess."

Levi boarded the vessel, knowing he had no time to waste. If Dani and Aaron got to the harbor and into a vehicle there, there was no way Levi would be able to catch up. His only chance to protect Dani was to get to her now.

Levi guided the boat away from the dock before speeding across the water.

"Good luck!" Jason called.

Levi would need more than luck. He needed backup.

He'd called Grant and Dash. They were on their way. He'd instructed them to call police on the mainland as well. They needed to monitor the public harbor on the other side of the water, just in case Levi couldn't catch up with the boat in time.

Levi couldn't wait for Grant and Dash to show up.

He had to get to Dani now.

As the boat zipped across the water, Levi scanned the horizon. The other boat had headed north—which was strange.

He didn't know of any harbors up this way. But sometimes, shallow spots popped up in the sound which meant there wasn't a straight line to get where you were going. Levi hadn't questioned it at the time.

Right now, everything seemed suspicious.

His back muscles tightened, and he threw the throttle wide open.

Levi had to find Dani. He didn't know all the details about what was going on, but he knew enough to know she was in danger. Somehow, Aaron had managed to pose as her boyfriend and even pass the background checks. Levi would figure that out later.

Dani was Mr. Wilkes's granddaughter. Someone wanted the land she'd inherited and would go through whatever means necessary to get it—even if that meant killing her.

They'd already killed Paul Robinson. They may have even killed Mr. Wilkes.

The rest of the details Levi would fill in later.

Lightning flashed in the distance.

That storm was coming in faster than he'd anticipated.

Levi's gut clenched again.

It appeared that everything just might be working against him right now.

CHAPTER FORTY-EIGHT

"I DIDN'T WANT to do any of this." Aaron's breathing was heavier and sweat spread across his skin as he turned toward Dani. The way his pupils dilated made him look... dangerous.

Terror rushed through Dani.

She squeezed her eyes shut and then flung them back open as more fragments of her past tried to form. Her gaze locked on Aaron's.

She wasn't going to make this easy on him. If he intended on hurting her, she would fight him with everything inside her.

"Aaron's not your real name, is it?" Dani licked her dry lips as she waited for his answer. The man frowned and shook his head, his meaty hands fisting and unfisting at his sides. "You've got to understand that things were never supposed to happen like this."

"Who's the real Aaron Demoss?"

"You did go on a few dates with him. Nothing serious . . . but he died in a mugging a couple of weeks ago."

Dani's throat tightened. "You did it, didn't you?"

His face tightened in complacency before he blurted, "I had no choice."

She scooted backward, her head throbbing. This man was a cold-blooded killer. And she was trapped on this boat with him. "I don't understand . . . why do you want me dead?"

"All you had to do was sign the property over." He ran a hand over his face as his pupils continued to dilate. "Everything would have been over with. But you had to get suspicious. That's when everything fell apart."

"What property?" He wasn't making sense. Yet something about his words teased at the cusp of her understanding.

"Mr. Wilkes's. You're his granddaughter."

Dani's lungs tightened as she absorbed that information. "Who would I have signed the property over to? You?"

The man's cheeks reddened. "You don't want to know. No one sees his face. Only me."

Another flashback hit Dani. An image of her walking across a sandy beach with two men. They'd been laughing together. An underlying sense of excitement had filled her.

Then something had gone wrong.

Her head pounded harder as she struggled to remember more details.

Her gaze flashed back up to the man posing as Aaron. "Why is that land so important?"

"It means money. A lot of money."

"Did you kill the man found on the island?"

"I was going to it, but the horse did it for me. Paul realized what was going on and got suspicious. He was going to ruin our whole plan. None of this would have happened if you hadn't decided to hire your own lawyer."

The hole in the pit of Dani's stomach continued to grow. "And Skeeter? Are you the one who tied him up?"

"I had to create a distraction for authorities on the island. Tying the horse up just made sense."

"I don't understand . . ." Even though pieces of the puzzle were forming, Dani still couldn't put them together.

"I brought you to the island at your request. You wanted to see the land before you sold it. We decided to humor you. But when you saw the property, you changed your mind. Said you wanted to keep it as part of your history." The man's nostrils flared. "That's when I had to take drastic measures."

"So you killed the real Aaron Demoss *and* Mr. Wilkes?" Dani was keeping count—that was at least two people who'd died at the hands of the man in front of her.

Aaron—or whatever his real name was—pressed his lips together, his entire face seeming to tremble with emotion. Anger? Maybe. Frustration. Definitely. Regret? Quite possibly.

"I didn't want to do any of it. I had no choice. Like I don't have any choice right now."

As wind swept over the boat, Dani swung her gaze to the horizon. The storm was practically here. The front had moved more quickly than any of them had guessed.

If they didn't get to the harbor soon, she'd be in trouble—in more ways than one.

Dani glanced at the boat captain. The man didn't even turn to look at Aaron or Dani. He only stared straight ahead. He was in on this too, wasn't he? Paid to look away? To pretend he didn't see?

The sickly feeling in her stomach only grew stronger.

She flinched as another flashback hit her—a memory of a man standing in front of her with a gun as a storm raged around them.

I'm sorry, Dani.

Her gaze shot back to Aaron. No, not Aaron. That wasn't his real name.

It was ... "Bobby?"

His face reddened. "I really wish you hadn't remembered, Dani. Things were a lot less complicated when you had amnesia. But I suppose that all good things must come to an end."

LEVI SPOTTED the boat in the distance.

Just as he laid eyes on it, another streak of lightning flashed in the sky, and the wind kicked up.

He didn't have much time.

The storm would be on them soon.

As Levi came closer, Aaron looked back, as if he heard the roar of Levi's motor.

The other boat seemed to kick up speed.

"That's not going to work," Levi muttered, his teeth grinding together in determination.

He knew these waters better than anyone. He wasn't afraid to prove that.

The engine buzzed as he charged forward.

Levi's cell rang again. It was Grant.

"What's going on?" Levi shoved the device between his ear and shoulder.

"We're on our way to help you," Grant said. "But first, I thought I'd let you know that Aaron Demoss died three weeks ago in a mysterious mugging. The person who did it still hasn't been caught."

"What?" Levi shouldn't be surprised. But he was.

He'd sent Aaron's picture to Dani's friend,

Carolyn. Had she been a plant, someone who was working with the bad guys all along? It was the only thing that made sense.

Levi had been set up.

"I ran this man's photo through the system," Grant continued. "He's not a lawyer. In fact, his real name is Bobby Fleming. He's a career criminal who's done jail time for assault and battery, armed robbery, and drug possession, among other things. Be careful."

"I will. I'm headed north, trying to catch them before the storm." As Levi said the words, another gust of wind swept over the water. The Currituck Sound, once placid, was now full of whitecaps that rocked the boat. No doubt a small craft advisory had been issued.

His muscles tightened.

No one should be out on the water in a thunderstorm.

But there was no way Levi was going back.

Not when Dani was in danger.

CHAPTER FORTY-NINE

"YOU DON'T HAVE to do this," Dani told Bobby.

She glanced around, looking for anything that might serve as a weapon. There was nothing, not even a fire extinguisher or an oar.

Had all those things been removed, just in case something like this happened?

"But I do." Bobby rubbed his fist as if preparing to use it. "Too many people are already dead. They'll keep dying until I finish this."

"Bobby . . ." How could Dani get through to him? All she had right now were her words . . . and, without her memory, they failed her.

"You were always nice to me. That's why I'm so sorry things have to end this way. I thought I'd finished you off the first time."

Another flashback hit Dani, and she flinched.

Her lungs froze as vivid memories assaulted her, making her feel like she was back in the line of fire.

She took a deep breath, trying to control her breathing as she stared at Bobby. "You shot me on the boat. I fell into the water. You left me for dead."

He frowned. "I tried to make it as painless as possible. I don't know how you survived. I can't make that same mistake this time. If I do, Carson will—"

"Who's Carson?" Should she know that man?

Bobby's face softened—but just for a minute. "My son. He's three. If I don't do the Captain's bidding, he'll..."

He didn't have to finish the statement. Dani knew. Whoever the Captain was, he would kill Bobby's son unless Bobby killed Dani.

"There's got to be a better way," Dani murmured. "Let's talk this through."

"There's not. Believe me. I've thought about it. Examined every angle. Tried to come up with another plan. This is the way it has to be, Dani."

Dani's eyes widened when Bobby pulled a gun from his waistband. "No . . . you don't have to do this."

His neck muscles tightened as he offered an apologetic frown. "But I do."

Dani couldn't just stand here as if she was powerless.

But she could only think of one way out of this situation.

Before she could second-guess herself, Dani dove into the raging waters behind her.

She'd take her chances: death by water or death by bullet.

"NO!" Levi saw Dani jump into the water.

He had to get to her. Between her injured arm, the rough water, and the approaching storm, her chances of surviving... he couldn't think about it.

He just needed to act.

As Levi raced her way, a bullet flew through the air.

Bobby had seen him and was shooting.

Levi crouched behind the console, using it as a shield from any more oncoming bullets. But he didn't slow down. He couldn't.

He kept his eyes on Dani's bobbing head. Once she was safe on his boat, he'd get her off this water, somewhere the storm couldn't hurt her.

But that was going to be easier said than done.

Another bullet pierced the air.

Levi was almost to Dani. Only twenty feet away.

But the other boat had turned around.

The vessel zoomed toward Dani.

Levi held his breath. It was going to be close. The other boat could get to her first.

His jaw clenched at the thought.

As Levi whizzed closer, the other boat appeared to clip Dani's head.

She disappeared under water.

Dear Lord ... no!

CHAPTER FIFTY

AS BLACKNESS SURROUNDED HER, memories battered Dani.

Her life clearly materialized in her mind, almost as if Play had been hit on a video.

She recoiled with horror as she remembered meeting Bobby. He'd come to her door one day and told her he was a lawyer for her grandfather's estate. He had all the paperwork to seem official.

Though his appearance had seemed unconventional, he'd been well-spoken and polite. He'd told Dani he'd been looking for her for a week. He gave her some history about her grandfather.

Her mom and dad had passed away, so Dani couldn't ask their opinions.

Bobby had also said there was a great offer on the land. He tried to convince her to sell. Made it seem like taking the offer was the smart thing to do and that she wouldn't have to worry about money for a while.

She'd almost signed right then. After all, her car had recently broken down and she had some water damage in her condo. She needed that money.

But, at the last minute, she'd hired her own lawyer.

Paul Robinson.

She'd asked to go see the land before signing. After all, the property and the house there was one of the only connections to her past. Would she be a fool to sell just so she could be more financially secure? Bobby had obliged.

As soon as she'd seen the island, she changed her mind. Bobby had become irate. Pushy.

Paul had told him to back off.

Bobby had pulled out a gun on the dark, sandy streets of Cape Corral. No one else had been around—except for a harem of horses.

Bobby had directed them toward the creatures. Told Paul to get on his knees.

He hadn't expected the horse to buck and kick him.

The blow had been fatal.

Bobby had mumbled something about nature making things easier for him.

Then he forced Dani to bury the man in the sand as he'd held a gun on her.

Afterward, they'd gone back to the boat. Though it began storming outside, he'd directed the captain out into the ocean and . . .

Dani's eyes flung open. Present-day reality hit her.

Air.

She needed air.

Arms tugged at her.

But whose arms were they? Bobby, who'd try to ensure she was dead? Or Levi, who'd rescue her?

Dani didn't know.

She surfaced and coughed, trying to tread water, to clear the blurriness from her eyes.

It was no use.

She was going to go under again. Her throbbing head made it impossible to think clearly. Her arm, bound in front of her, made it hard to stay afloat.

Lightning flashed in the distance as another wave engulfed her head.

"Dani, are you okay?"

Levi. That was Levi's voice. He was in the water. With her.

But she hardly had time to revel in either the sound or the realization.

Another bullet flew at them and thunder rumbled overhead.

"I'm going to get you to safety." Levi wrapped an arm around her waist. "Stay with me, okay?"

Dani kicked her legs beneath the water.

She'd do her best. But she was feeling weak. So, so weak.

LEVI HEARD another bullet hit the water.

As he sucked in another breath, a wave lapped over him, trying to push him and Dani into the depths of the Currituck Sound.

That wasn't an option.

He had to keep Dani above the water.

But he also had to keep her away from those bullets.

He glanced in the distance and saw Bobby's boat charging toward them.

They didn't have much time to make a move. Soon, it would be too late.

He glanced back. Levi's own boat had drifted. He hadn't had time to anchor it.

He didn't think he could make it back in time.

That left him only the option of going under.

"Can you hold your breath?" Levi asked Dani, watching her expression. Her eyelids pulled down, her face looked pale, and her breaths were entirely too shallow.

"I . . . I think so."

Levi worried about her. She looked so weak.

But they didn't have a lot of choices here.

"I'm going to be with you the whole time." Levi wiped the moisture from his face as another wave hit. "I won't let anything happen to you. Do you understand?"

She nodded, but the action was lackluster.

"On the count of three, we're going under. Okay?"

"Okay," she muttered.

"One. Two. Three." With one hand gripping hers, they dove under the water. They had to get away from these guys before they both ended up dead.

As quickly as Levi could, he swam toward his boat. His plan was to go underneath the skiff and pop up on the other side. The water was dark enough that they should be able to conceal their location—for a few minutes, at least.

Levi glanced beside him.

He could hardly see Dani in the murky water. But she looked okay. Her legs knifed through the water as her uninjured arm stroked forward.

Not much farther.

The shadow of the boat passed overhead.

Levi's lungs burned. He needed air.

Dani had to feel the burn also.

Finally, he pushed them to the surface and sucked in a deep breath.

But as he turned around, he spotted Bobby Fleming standing above him.

His gun was aimed right at Dani.

CHAPTER FIFTY-ONE

DANI'S RELIEF turned into terror.

Bobby stood above them.

His gun pointed at her.

She and Levi couldn't get out of this. It would be impossible.

She glanced at Levi, desperate to express to him how grateful she was that he'd tried to help. But they were in a no-win situation.

"You should have just made this easy," Bobby grumbled, cocking his weapon.

"You don't have to do this, Bobby," Levi said as he treaded water, one arm still on Dani.

"I don't have any choice. He's going to kill my son if I don't."

"Who's going to kill your son?" Levi asked. "Warren Wilhelmina?"

Bobby's face flushed. "It's not important. I don't

want to do this. I just wanted you both to know that. I didn't want to do any of this."

"Then don't," Dani said. "There has to be another way."

"There's not. I've thought it through. I don't have any other choice."

"Bobby, please." Dani stared at him. "I trusted you at one time. It's not too late."

Surprise washed over Levi's face. "You remember?"

She nodded. "I do. Everything."

When they got out of this, they'd have a lot to talk about.

But first, they had to get out of this.

Bobby's gun trembled in his hand. "Even more reason why we need to end this."

Dani braced herself for the pain she knew was about to come. Because there was nothing to shield her from Bobby's bullet.

Only water.

LEVI SHOVED Dani behind him as another wave nearly pulled them under. Thunder rumbled across the sky. The storm was almost on them.

"You're going to be discovered, and you're going to go to jail," Levi said, desperate to keep Bobby talking until backup arrived. "It's just a matter of time."

"You don't know that."

"I do," Levi said. "You won't get away with this."

Bobby ran a hand over his face. "I'm going to do this and then run. It's the only choice I have."

"You always have choices," Dani said.

"No, I don't!" Spittle shot from his mouth. "It's why I had to kill Paul. Aaron. Mr. Wilkes."

Levi's muscles tightened at his words. Three dead bodies. This man definitely wouldn't hesitate to add two more to his list.

"What did Paul do?" Levi asked.

"He tried to backstab us and get this land for himself. He wasn't working for us. He was working for himself."

So there were other people involved. Who was the other man who was a part of this?

Levi would have to think about that later. His best guess was that Mr. Wilhelmina had put him up to this.

"It was nice knowing you, Dani." Bobby extended his arm, regret claiming his features.

Just as Levi had braced himself to take action, a voice cut through the air.

"Police! Put your hands up!"

A new watercraft appeared on the other side of the boat.

Grant and Dash.

Levi watched Bobby carefully, unsure how he would react. Would he shoot anyway? Or comply?

His face twisted with uncertainty. Then he turned the gun toward himself.

"Think of Carson," Dani yelled.

Bobby shook his head, color filling his skin. "He's not going to want anything to do with me. I'm a no-good loser, just like his mom tells him."

"You don't know that he won't want anything to do with you. You're his father. You can make things right—but only if you're alive."

"It's too late for me." Bobby raised his gun again.

"It's never too late," Dani called. "You've done bad things, but I can tell you still have a conscience."

Grant boarded the boat and took the gun from Bobby.

He didn't resist. Instead, his shoulders slumped as Grant handcuffed him.

The boat captain dove into the water. Dash dove in after him, surfacing with the man only seconds later.

"I was just hired to drive the boat," the man said between gulps of water. "I don't have anything to do with this."

"We'll let the court decide that," Grant muttered.

Another boat pulled up on the other side of them. The Coast Guard.

A few minutes later, they lifted Dani and Levi onboard. They placed blankets around them as they took them back to dry land.

It looked like this storm might really be over and that shelter was in sight.

CHAPTER FIFTY-TWO

TWO WEEKS LATER

DANI BRIGHTENED when she heard the knock at the door. She rose from the couch at the inn and rushed to answer.

A smile lit her face when she spotted Levi standing on the porch with some wildflowers in his hands.

"For you." He stepped closer and wrapped his arms around her. "Good morning."

"It is a good morning." She was alive and well and back in Cape Corral. Emmy had let her stay at the inn. And Levi . . . he had hardly left her side since everything went down.

What was there to complain about?

Levi scooted back just enough to plant a quick kiss on Dani's lips before murmuring,

"You ready for this?"

Dani nodded, even though a quell of nerves fluttered in her stomach. "I am."

He extended his hand. "Let's go then."

She laced her fingers with his.

Levi was accompanying her as she visited a lawyer on the mainland. Today, Grandfather Wilkes's property would officially become hers.

The past two weeks had been a whirlwind.

Bobby had been arrested and charged with murder, among other things. His son was safe and with Bobby's ex-wife. Apparently, the man had gotten himself straight—until, in a moment of weakness, he'd taken a shot of heroin. When his wife found out, she left him and took his son with her.

Though their relationship was strained, that little boy had been Bobby's main motivator. He couldn't let anything happen to his son.

Someone else had known that and used him as leverage.

The driver of the boat had also been arrested, though he appeared to just be a hired hand who'd been paid to stay out of things.

A third man was now in custody—someone named Stanley Becker. He was believed to be the one who'd ordered the hits. The man was a real estate developer who'd been known for doing some shady deals.

Levi hadn't been able to find any link between

Stanley and Warren Wilhelmina, though he suspected the two were connected. Warren claimed to know nothing about the turn of events. Levi would continue looking into him, however.

Carolyn Thomas had also been arrested. She was one of Dani's coworkers, but she'd fallen into debt from too much shopping and was on the verge of losing her house.

Bobby had somehow discovered that and exploited it. He'd paid Carolyn to lie for him. The computer guru had also helped him manipulate some online files that made it appear that Aaron Demoss looked like Bobby. She'd scrubbed the internet of any articles about his death. She'd photoshopped some images of Dani with Bobby, to make it look like they'd really been together.

And now she was facing criminal charges.

Finally, the danger seemed to have subsided for Dani.

After the whirlwind of being rescued, watching Bobby be arrested, and being rushed to the hospital with a possible concussion, Dani had taken Levi with her back to her home in Chesterfield. The space confirmed that she'd been a young professional woman. She had indeed casually dated Aaron Demoss.

When Aaron had heard she'd inherited some land, he began to investigate. When he did, he'd ended up dead.

Though Dani mourned his loss, the two of them hadn't been far enough along in their relationship to feel any deep, heart-wrenching grief. Mostly she regretted that his involvement with her had led to his death.

It turned out she truly was Ed Wilkes's granddaughter, and he'd left her his land and the quaint house on it. There was no way she'd sell either—not just because of the easement but because that place was a part of her family's history. She only wished she'd had a chance to get to know her grandfather.

"So, did you decide what you want to do?" Levi asked as they pulled up to the lawyer's office.

She offered a resolute nod. "I'm staying in Cape Corral. In my grandfather's house."

A smile tugged at Levi's lips. "Are you sure? That's going to be a big change for you."

"I'm positive. I've fallen in love with this place. I can't imagine leaving." She would live in her grandfather's house. Her old job would allow her to work from home.

"That makes me happy to hear." He leaned closer, his eyes warm with affection.

"I'm glad that makes you happy." Whenever Levi looked at her like that, Dani felt like lava flowed through her blood. The feeling was divine. "You know what else makes me happy? The fact that you didn't take that job in Maine."

"I've got everything I want right here." Slowly, he leaned forward and planted a long, lingering kiss on her lips.

When Levi pulled back, Dani couldn't stop grinning.

He held out his hand. "You ready to make this move official?"

Dani nodded as she slipped her hand into his. "I am . . . cowboy."

He grinned. "Then what do you say we go make some new memories together?"

"I say that sounds perfect."

~~~

Thank you for reading Saltwater Cowboy. If you enjoyed this book, would you leave a review? Reviews truly do help authors and we appreciate them!

Stay tuned for book two, **Breakwater Protector**, coming October 2020.

If you haven't signed up for my newsletter yet, please do so here: www.christybarritt.com.

COMPLETE BOOK LIST

Squeaky Clean Mysteries:
- #1 Hazardous Duty
- #2 Suspicious Minds
- #2.5 It Came Upon a Midnight Crime (novella)
- #3 Organized Grime
- #4 Dirty Deeds
- #5 The Scum of All Fears
- #6 To Love, Honor and Perish
- #7 Mucky Streak
- #8 Foul Play
- #9 Broom & Gloom
- #10 Dust and Obey
- #11 Thrill Squeaker
- #11.5 Swept Away (novella)
- #12 Cunning Attractions
- #13 Cold Case: Clean Getaway
- #14 Cold Case: Clean Sweep

#15 Cold Case: Clean Break
#16 Cleans to an End (coming soon)
While You Were Sweeping, A Riley Thomas Spinoff

The Sierra Files:
#1 Pounced
#2 Hunted
#3 Pranced
#4 Rattled

The Gabby St. Claire Diaries (a Tween Mystery series):
The Curtain Call Caper
The Disappearing Dog Dilemma
The Bungled Bike Burglaries

The Worst Detective Ever
#1 Ready to Fumble
#2 Reign of Error
#3 Safety in Blunders
#4 Join the Flub
#5 Blooper Freak
#6 Flaw Abiding Citizen
#7 Gaffe Out Loud
#8 Joke and Dagger
#9 Wreck the Halls
#10 Glitch and Famous (coming soon)

Raven Remington
    Relentless 1
    Relentless 2 (coming soon)

Holly Anna Paladin Mysteries:
    #1 Random Acts of Murder
    #2 Random Acts of Deceit
    #2.5 Random Acts of Scrooge
    #3 Random Acts of Malice
    #4 Random Acts of Greed
    #5 Random Acts of Fraud
    #6 Random Acts of Outrage
    #7 Random Acts of Iniquity

Lantern Beach Mysteries
    #1 Hidden Currents
    #2 Flood Watch
    #3 Storm Surge
    #4 Dangerous Waters
    #5 Perilous Riptide
    #6 Deadly Undertow

Lantern Beach Romantic Suspense
    Tides of Deception
    Shadow of Intrigue
    Storm of Doubt
    Winds of Danger
    Rains of Remorse

Lantern Beach P.D.
- On the Lookout
- Attempt to Locate
- First Degree Murder
- Dead on Arrival
- Plan of Action

Lantern Beach Escape
- Afterglow (a novelette)

Lantern Beach Blackout
- Dark Water
- Safe Harbor
- Ripple Effect
- Rising Tide

Crime á la Mode
- Deadman's Float
- Milkshake Up
- Bomb Pop Threat
- Banana Split Personalities

The Sidekick's Survival Guide
- The Art of Eavesdropping
- The Perks of Meddling
- The Exercise of Interfering
- The Practice of Prying
- The Skill of Snooping
- The Craft of Being Covert

Carolina Moon Series
- Home Before Dark
- Gone By Dark
- Wait Until Dark
- Light the Dark
- Taken By Dark

Suburban Sleuth Mysteries:
- Death of the Couch Potato's Wife

Fog Lake Suspense:
- Edge of Peril
- Margin of Error
- Brink of Danger
- Line of Duty

Cape Thomas Series:
- Dubiosity
- Disillusioned
- Distorted

Standalone Romantic Mystery:
- The Good Girl

Suspense:
- Imperfect
- The Wrecking

Sweet Christmas Novella:

Home to Chestnut Grove

Standalone Romantic-Suspense:
Keeping Guard
The Last Target
Race Against Time
Ricochet
Key Witness
Lifeline
High-Stakes Holiday Reunion
Desperate Measures
Hidden Agenda
Mountain Hideaway
Dark Harbor
Shadow of Suspicion
The Baby Assignment
The Cradle Conspiracy
Trained to Defend

Nonfiction:
Characters in the Kitchen
Changed: True Stories of Finding God through Christian Music (out of print)
The Novel in Me: The Beginner's Guide to Writing and Publishing a Novel (out of print)

ABOUT THE AUTHOR

USA Today has called Christy Barritt's books "scary, funny, passionate, and quirky."

Christy writes both mystery and romantic suspense novels that are clean with underlying messages of faith. Her books have won the Daphne du Maurier Award for Excellence in Suspense and Mystery, have been twice nominated for the Romantic Times Reviewers' Choice Award, and have finaled for both a Carol Award and Foreword Magazine's Book of the Year.

She is married to her Prince Charming, a man who thinks she's hilarious—but only when she's not trying to be. Christy is a self-proclaimed klutz, an avid music lover who's known for spontaneously bursting into song, and a road trip aficionado.

When she's not working or spending time with her family, she enjoys singing, playing the guitar, and exploring small, unsuspecting towns where people have no idea how accident-prone she is.

Find Christy online at:
www.christybarritt.com
www.facebook.com/christybarritt
www.twitter.com/cbarritt

Sign up for Christy's newsletter to get information on all of her latest releases here: **www.christybarritt.com/newsletter-sign-up/**

If you enjoyed this book, please consider leaving a review.

Made in the USA
Monee, IL
02 November 2021